CONTENTS

BOND & BOOK

The Long, Long Good-Bye of "The Last Bookstore"

Mizuki Nomura

ILLUSTRATION BY
Miho Takeoka

YEN ON

New York

BOND & BOOK
The Long, Long Good-Bye of "The Last Bookstore"

MIZUKI NOMURA

Translation by Nicole Wilder
Cover art by Miho Takeoka

MUSUBU TO HON. "SAIGO NO HONYASAN" NO NAGAINAGAI OWARI
©Mizuki Nomura 2020
First published in Japan in 2020 by KADOKAWA CORPORATION, Tokyo.
English translation rights arranged with KADOKAWA CORPORATION, Tokyo through
TUTTLE-MORI AGENCY, INC., Tokyo.

English translation © 2022 by Yen Press, LLC

Yen On
150 West 30th Street, 19th Floor
New York, NY 10001

Visit us at yenpress.com • facebook.com/yenpress • twitter.com/yenpress
yenpress.tumblr.com • instagram.com/yenpress

First Yen On Edition: January 2022

Yen On is an imprint of Yen Press, LLC.
The Yen On name and logo are trademarks of Yen Press, LLC.

The publisher is not responsible for websites (or their content) that are not owned by the publisher.

Library of Congress Cataloging-in-Publication Data
Names: Nomura, Mizuki, author. | Takeoka, Miho, illustrator. | Wilder, Nicole, translator.
Title: Bond and book. the long, long good-bye of "The Last Bookstore" / Mizuki Nomura ;
illustration by Miho Takeoka ; translation by Nicole Wilder.
Other titles: Musubu to Hon. "Gekashitsu" no ichizu. English
Description: First Yen On edition. | New York, NY : Yen On, 2021.
Identifiers: LCCN 2021023513 | ISBN 9781975325732 (v. 1 ; hardcover) |
ISBN 9781975325718 (v. 2 ; hardcover)
Subjects: CYAC: Books and reading—Fiction. | Magic—Fiction. |
Mystery and detective stories. | LCGFT: Novels.
Classification: LCC PZ7.N728 Bk 2021 | DDC [Fic]—dc23
LC record available at https://lccn.loc.gov/2021023513

ISBNs: 978-1-9753-2571-8 (hardcover)
978-1-9753-2572-5 (ebook)

10 9 8 7 6 5 4 3 2 1

LSC-C

Printed in the United States of America

"We tiny people can discern the contents of a letter without even opening the envelope. When we feel the letters, one that has nothing but blunt, plain things written in it will feel chilly, cold even. But the more emotional sentiment that was included in a letter, the warmer it will feel in the hand."

Excerpt from *The Long, Long Story of the Postman*

Prologue

A heavy snow was falling on the morning that Minami Tsuburaya learned that the owner of the bookstore where she worked part-time had passed away.

"I'm the last bookseller in this town, you know. So as long as I'm alive, I'll never close up shop."

That had recently become the favorite phrase of the store's owner and manager, Emon Koumoto, who would recite it while squinting his eyes behind his glasses in a kindly expression. Neither that smile nor his gentle tone of voice had conveyed the feeling of grim resolve that one might expect from such words. His attitude had always been bright and sunny.

Minami would smile, too, and respond with something like *"Well then, you'll have to live a nice long life."*

Ten years earlier, when Minami was still in middle school, there had been as many as five bookstores in town. But books were less popular now, and the rise of e-books and online booksellers had seen each store close one by one.

Koumoto Books, the last store standing, was a slim three-story building that occupied a quiet street alongside old cafés and bars near a small movie theater. Though it was in the opposite direction from the prosperous part of town, it was still a short three-minute walk from the station. Local booklovers flocked there to relax.

Even so, Minami was well aware that sales were down year over year, distributions were dwindling, and most of the big releases that the store worked hard to keep in stock for people who wanted to buy them at launch went unsold and had to be returned to the publishers. It was heart-wrenching.

But even then, the owner would smile calmly and say in his mellow voice, *"Koumoto Books is this town's last bookstore. If we disappear, I'm sure a lot of people will be sad and won't know what to do. It takes an hour by car to go to the bookstore in the next town, and many older people here find that difficult during the snowy season. So I want to keep this shop going for as long as I live."*

It had sounded as if he were saying *Close this shop over my dead body,* which had always made Minami feel secretly anxious.

...I wonder if the boss will remarry.

He's young, still in his forties, slim, a smart dresser, and he's outgoing and kind... I'm sure there are plenty of women who would like him.

But maybe he doesn't want to have a family again. Losing loved ones is tragic, especially the way he did. Really, it's not surprising he would think that way after such a depressing incident...

Just thinking about Koumoto Books facing its end alongside the owner's death is lonesome, like an icy frost gripping your heart.

Minami had reassured herself that it was still a long way off and had hoped for a future where the owner could have a new family that would continue to operate Koumoto Books.

She'd never imagined that the owner would pass away at the young age of forty-nine.

And in such an unnatural accident at that.

A college boy working part-time in the bookstore discovered the body. He said that when he'd arrived at the store at nine in the morning to prepare for opening at ten, the owner had been sprawled out in the children's book section on the second floor, with blood flowing from his head.

Next to him was an overturned stepladder. Books were scattered all around.

He must have stayed late the previous evening to do some organizing.

As he was shelving books, the stepladder had toppled out from under him. When he'd grabbed a shelf for stability, all the books had fallen in an avalanche onto his head, and one had hit him in a critical spot. Another blow to the head followed as he'd hit the corner of his cart, and by the time the blood had pooled on the floor, he had already stopped breathing.

The part-timer had called an ambulance in a panic, but it was already too late, and the police had deemed his death an unfortunate accident.

Mr. Koumoto had no living relatives. With the loss of its sole proprietor, the bookstore would have to close.

"Koumoto Books is closing? Where are we supposed to buy books now?"

"And it was so convenient, too, close to the station and with a good collection. The owner was so kind and knowledgeable."

"What an awful way to go out, especially because he was the third generation in his family to run the place. He kept giving his all for this town even after he lost his wife and child. That family had the worst luck."

"Can't they keep it open as 'Something-or-other Books'?"

"It just won't be the same here without it."

Many people expressed similar sentiments to Minami and the other staff at the bookstore, but no eccentric benefactor materialized to purchase the failing business and keep the store running. Thus, Koumoto Books, which had operated for sixty-nine years straight, was slated to close up shop on the last day of March, two months after the death of Emon Koumoto.

The shop had been shuttered since the accident, but before it closed for good, it would reopen for just one week to show appreciation for its customers and clear out the inventory. Minami was busy with the preparations.

She hadn't felt like doing anything for about a month after the owner passed away and had spent every day idling at home. Even crying was beyond her—the reality that the store owner was gone and that Koumoto

Books was going to disappear still felt far away. Minami had dulled her feelings to protect herself from heartache. She'd spent all day in bed with her eyes closed.

Like many booklovers, Minami was nearsighted and couldn't even see as far as her outstretched hand without her glasses. Nevertheless, she had stumbled around her apartment without putting them on and groped her way to the refrigerator to retrieve ham, cheese, and other foods that didn't require any preparation, which she begrudgingly ate out of obligation if not hunger. She'd spent several days like that.

Gradually, she'd managed to convince herself to get up and start moving, and now she was furiously working to prepare for the final week of business and stave off her depressing thoughts.

There were five part-timers at the store: Minami, two high schoolers, one college student, and one housewife. Minami had been working part-time at Koumoto Books for the last seven years, since her second year of high school. She had been there the longest of any of her coworkers, so they were relying on her to see things through. Plus, since she wasn't studying or taking care of a family like the others, she could spend all her time preparing for the shop's last hurrah.

That's how she ended up at the store alone again, finishing up some small details.

Once she finished tidying up the comics corner on the third floor, she headed down the stairs.

From the children's section on the second floor, she heard a voice.

Someone was speaking, even though she had already drawn the shutters down and should have been the only person in the store.

Maybe one of the part-timers came back for something?

From her position midway down the stairs, Minami lifted her glasses up just a little bit and strained to scan the second floor.

As she gazed around the room, she saw an unfamiliar young man standing in front of some shelves.

Is that a high schooler?

The intruder had a slight build and wore a navy-blue duffel coat with a white scarf wrapped around his neck.

Minami started to approach the trespasser, ready to scold him for entering the store without permission, when she heard his somewhat high-pitched, boyish voice again.

"Is that so? Mm-hmm…it's so tragic that happened. Hmm…I understand."

Who is he talking to?
But no matter what angle she held her glasses at, the only person Minami could see was the young man in the duffel coat.

"All right, I'm sorry, Princess Yonaga. This isn't cheating, I promise. After all, you insisted on coming along no matter what when I told you to stay home."

Minami was starting to feel uneasy.
Who was the boy talking to?

"You're right—ten days is too long to be apart. I feel the same way. Yes, I love you. No, I'm not lying. You're the only one for me. So please just quiet down a little. I swear a million times to the god of books, I'm not cheating on you."

The boy was standing exactly where the store owner had collapsed and died.
When Minami realized that, she felt all the hair on the back of her neck stand up and her limbs stiffen.

"Sorry for the interruption. My girlfriend is very cute, but she's the jealous type. Let's see, then. I'll ask again—*who killed Emon?*"

Her shoulders hitched slightly in surprise, as if someone had run a cold hand across her spine. Unable to endure the creeping fear that hit her all at once, she shouted angrily, "What are you doing over there?!"
The boy turned around.
His large glasses gave him an innocent look. Mouth slightly agape, he stared back at Minami with big, round eyes.

As he moved, his black hair bounced softly—he seemed like a totally unremarkable schoolboy.

In fact, his appearance was so ordinary that Minami eased up. Her fear faded, and she approached him without hesitation.

"Who were you talking to just now? You said something about the boss, didn't you? What's the meaning of this?" she asked, scowling.

The boy blinked rapidly behind his glasses and put both hands up, either to stop her or to gesture in surrender.

"I'm sorry. I called out from the back door downstairs, but no one answered, so I let myself in. My name is Musubu Enoki. I came here after I received a notice from a lawyer."

Young Musubu didn't sound as though he was from the area. He spoke like someone you'd see on TV, without an accent of any sort.

Did this kid come from another city?

And what's this about a lawyer?

What he told her next only strengthened Minami's suspicion of him.

"Apparently, there was something written about me in the will that Mr. Emon left with his lawyer before he died. In the event that he passed away, I'm supposed to be entrusted with all the books in here."

He continued with a friendly, unguarded smile on his face.

"I've just started spring break, you see. From tomorrow on, I'll be working with you for a little while. Let's see—you're Minami Tsuburaya, right? The one who's been working here the longest out of all the part-timers and the most reliable lady around! Wow, how reassuring! I'm used to taking care of books, but this will be my first time working in a bookstore, so I'm sure I'll be depending on you!"

Book
1

*The Field
Guide of
Extinct
Animals*
Was
Waiting

"Come on in! Starting today, we're having our grand store closing! We've got all sorts of activities! You can take commemorative photographs with your favorite books, make a sign to display, and more! Please come join us!"

The young man in glasses, wearing a white shirt and a blue apron with the store's name printed on it, was shouting clearly and energetically at passersby. Minami watched with a stern look in her eye.

"Hello, everyone, I'm Musubu Enoki. I'll be here at Koumoto Books helping out until the store closes. It's just a short while, but I look forward to working with you!"

It was the day after Minami had met him.

None of the other part-timers had been able to hide their bewilderment at the small boy greeting them with a smile, either.

Starting in April, he would be in his second year of high school. He had gone out of his way to come from his home in Tokyo to this small town in Tohoku. The owner of the store had written in his will that upon his death, all the volumes in Koumoto Books were to be entrusted to Musubu Enoki. Minami had heard that from both Musubu and a lawyer who had visited the shop the day before.

He didn't "bequeath" the books, he "entrusted" them—what does that mean?

As long as it was within a set window of time, the store could return books stocked by a distributor. New releases would typically be sent back for resale, so Minami had figured the same would happen with most of the leftover books.

So what was the boss thinking, leaving that up to the discretion of a high school boy?

In any case, if this boy had the right to every book in the store, that meant they couldn't sell anything without his permission. But where did that leave the closing sale?

All the staff had been concerned, but Musubu had bowed and spoken to them with a sincere smile.

"Ah, the books here belong to the shop until the very end, so don't worry. We'll hold a grand store closing as planned; everything will be fine. And I'll be here to help out."

His smile betrayed not a trace of ill will. For the time being, all the part-timers besides Minami seemed to be put at ease.

"But what kind of relationship did you think Enoki had with Emon anyway? Were they related?"

"I heard that the boss's family all died; he's not supposed to have any relatives left."

"Maybe he had a secret love child!"

"Now that you mention it, he does wear glasses… There's a resemblance!"

Minami scolded the part-timers.

"They just wear similar-looking big glasses, that's all! There's no way the boss would have a secret kid."

Since coming back to work at the bookshop, Minami would often find herself on edge, even at the best of times. When she looked at Musubu's friendly face, she couldn't help but feel a sting of irritation and suspicion in her chest.

She couldn't understand why the boss had entrusted all the books in the shop to Musubu, who was still just a high schooler. It frustrated her—she had been working there the longest and had been his most reliable employee.

Why'd he give everything to this kid?

He's not even a local—he's from Tokyo.

She glumly repeated this to herself like a refrain.

Hearing him talk about his relationship with Emon only made her more annoyed.

"I happened to make his acquaintance last autumn, when he came to Tokyo on business. I'm a booklover, too, so we hit it off, and that's all there is to it."

Last autumn?! They'd only known each other for half a year! I've been working here for seven.

Moreover, on the first day they had met, he had been muttering to himself in front of the bookshelf where Emon had died. That had been bothering her ever since and had sent her deeper into uncertainty.

"Who killed Emon?"

That was what he'd asked back then.

When Minami had asked him what he meant by it, he'd played dumb.

"Uh…are you sure I said that?"

"You definitely did. I heard you myself."

When Minami had pressed in closer, the boy's eyes had widened, and he'd let out a little shriek.

*   *   *

"I-I'm not ch-cheating, Princess Yonaga. My heart can't take it when you suddenly start 'cursing' me, so cut it out, please. Yes, of course it's a misunderstanding. I love you, so quit with the curses."

Musubu got flustered without warning and started talking to himself again.

Minami stared at him, dumbfounded, while he apologized.

"Sorry, my girlfriend gets super jealous whenever I even talk to or approach another girl, so do you think you could back off a little?"

"Your girlfriend? Where is she, then? You've been talking to yourself this whole time. Frankly, you seem kinda crazy."

When she asked about this girlfriend, his eyes darted around guiltily behind his glasses.

"I try my best not to talk to her in front of other people, but it just sort of happened. Um, the thing is, I can talk to books."

He was blurting out something that didn't make any sense again.

"Are you playing some kind of prank?"

"No, of course not! It's true. For whatever reason, I've always been able to hear the voices of books. And when I talk to them, they answer me willingly. When I mention my girlfriend, I'm talking about her.*"*

From the pocket of his duffel coat, he excitedly pulled out a thin paperback book with a blue cover.

Princess Yonaga and Ear Man.

That's a novel by Ango Sakaguchi.

If I remember correctly, it's the story of a sculptor who is tormented by a beautiful and devilish girl who loves to watch people die. That's right—Princess Yonaga is the name of that malicious young lady.

Is this like how boys who are fans of light novels and manga will often call their favorite heroine their "wife"?

But he says he's actually conversing with this "princess." Either he's a serious otaku, or puberty is making him crazy.

"Princess Yonaga is greeting you, too, Ms. Tsuburaya. She's saying, 'If you put your face close to Musubu's or touch him or wink at him, I'll curse you'... Sorry, but it would help me out if you'd be careful."

There's no way I'm gonna wink at you!

Was he deliberately trying to change the subject from what happened to the shop owner to make her angry? She was suspicious—then realized something and jumped with alarm.

"Did you just call me Tsuburaya? How do you know my name? And earlier...you knew I was the most senior employee here."

Yeah, you said that I had been working here the longest and that I seemed to be the most reliable, didn't you?

"Who *did you hear that from?*"

When she asked this question, he looked at her intently with big, clear eyes from behind his transparent lenses and smiled as he answered.

"The books told me."

How ridiculous.

Despite her misgivings, for a moment Minami almost deluded herself into believing Musubu could really hear the voices of books. But when she gave it some more thought, she realized he must have seen her personnel file beforehand. Her photograph would have even been attached to her résumé.

Surely that's how he had known who she was.

There was no way he could have conversed with the books.

If Musubu believed that he could, he was either loopy from hormones or suffering from delusions of grandeur.

"Who killed Emon?"

When he'd said that, he'd sounded as if he'd been speaking to someone from a reality of his own creation.

As Minami helped a steady stream of customers, she occasionally shot a pointed glance in his direction.

He was working hard, calling out to customers and handling them well. Chiding herself to worry about doing her own job before saying anything about him, she tried to channel her annoyance into her work.

Positive attitude aside, Musubu had said he was used to handling books, but his manner was so delicate, it was astonishing. He touched them softly, as if he were cradling a precious treasure, and slipped on their paper covers gently, as if caressing them. And when he looked at a book, it was with eyes as affectionate as when you gaze at a dear friend.

Whenever a customer picked up a book or went to make a purchase, his lips curled into a contented smile.

The way he was acting made her recall Emon, the owner—he, too, would look genuinely happy whenever someone purchased a book. He would smile softly as he saw the volume off, as if he were silently indicating he was glad for it.

But Emon and Musubu are different people, and there's absolutely no way he's the boss's secret kid!

"Looks like we should have prepared a bit more colored paper for the customers to make signs, huh? I'll get right on that."

Musubu wore a more carefree expression than Emon ever had.

As he was cutting the colorful poster board into different shapes, Musubu asked, "You got the idea to have customers make and display these pop signs from that book, right? *A Funeral for Kanoyama Books*...?" He sounded as if he were enjoying himself.

"A bestseller depicting the only bookstore in a small, snowy village in the last days before its closing. People with a connection to the shop come to visit one after another, and the pictures they take with their favorite books are displayed throughout the shop with pride and joy, like multicolored flags—that scene was incredibly striking in both the novel and the movie. The author, Kouichi Tamogami, is apparently from this town. He held a book signing at Koumoto Books."

"...Mr. Tamogami was... Before his debut, he was a regular here, and I heard he was close friends with Emon, so..."

With a smash-hit movie on his hands, the bestselling author had held a book signing in this small local bookstore. The news had excited the townspeople, and on the day of the signing, a long line had stretched out of the building.

Everyone had been clutching a copy of *A Funeral for Kanoyama Books* to their chest, and Emon had been smiling effusively as he chatted with the crowd.

Undoubtedly, it had been Koumoto Books's finest hour.

The internet wasn't as widespread as it is now, there were no smart-phones, and there were fewer ways to amuse oneself alone, so for many people, reading books was a pleasure, a blessing, even a reason to live.

The heavy weight of a finely bound hardcover in the hand, the feel of the crisp new pages that threatened to slice one's fingers...they were enough to make the heart flutter with anticipation.

That was nearly twenty years ago.

At the time, Minami hadn't even started kindergarten yet, but she remembered standing in the long line with her mother and getting the author to sign the inside cover of their book.

It had gotten lost before she knew it, though.

"Do you think Mr. Tamogami will come to our grand store closing? He's supposed to come, right? Well, if he does, it'll be amazing publicity. Just imagine, an author who wrote a bestseller about the final days of his village's only bookshop, and he's coming to the grand send-off of the last bookstore in *this* town," Musubu babbled. His springy black hair bounced and bobbed as he spoke.

"I wonder... I did contact him, but he's a busy man."

Though Kouichi Tamogami's popularity had declined since his heyday, he still periodically published new works.

Since he had held a signing at Koumoto Books only once and declined all further invitations, even for giving lectures at the local community center, he probably wasn't coming.

At one point, when sales had started to decline, someone had suggested asking him to return for another book signing, but Emon had narrowed his eyes behind his glasses and smiled sadly as he answered.

"Hmm... Mr. Tamogami might be...difficult to get ahold of."

In the days when Mr. Tamogami was living in town, he and Emon had been close enough friends that he would sometimes spend all night chatting with him in the bookstore's office. But that closeness must have faded after Mr. Tamogami had gotten famous and moved to Tokyo.

An old part-timer who had quit the year before had mentioned it to Minami.

"When Emon's baby was born, a congratulatory present arrived from Mr. Tamogami, and Emon was overjoyed. But when he called him up to say thank you and asked him to come back and visit Koumoto Books sometime, he apparently turned him down... Emon was really sad about it.

"Emon's not the type to wear his troubles on his sleeve, but...I remember it well. First because he seemed really unhappy, and second because he actually complained about it, which was something he rarely ever did."

He'd griped about Mr. Tamogami being coldhearted, even though the two of them had been such good friends. They'd found time to hang out in the office together even when Emon had been busy. But I guess it was inevitable.

People who move away always forget where they came from...

But the people who stay always remember the ones who left, gossiping as if they'd seen them just yesterday.

*   *   *

"Huh...look at that customer."

Musubu, whose hands had been practically flying at the register as they had been chatting, stopped abruptly. He stared at the door, concerned about something.

Wide and round behind his lenses, his eyes were wavering as they followed the movements of one particular customer.

Past the register, down an aisle.

And beyond.

He was holding his breath and straining to hear something. Only his eyes moved, swaying like a single leaf floating on the water's surface.

"Minami, is that guy a regular customer?"

"Uh...I don't know him, but..."

"Is that...so...?"

Musubu seemed really worried about him for some reason, so Minami strained to get a look. He was an old man, with white hair and a slightly bent back.

Was he in his midseventies, maybe?

Deep wrinkles were carved in sharp relief on his face, and his eyes were sunken. He seemed impatient for some reason. Minami could sense his irritation by the look in his eye and the pace of his gait, and it caused her to shudder.

Anyone who works at a bookstore for a long time will be able to identify shoplifters.

Recently, it hadn't been just young kids—older people who were struggling to make ends meet had been turning to shoplifting, too.

Looking carefully at the coat the man was wearing, she could see that the hem and sleeves were starting to fray with age.

Maybe...

Musubu was still silently lost in thought. Leaving him behind, Minami began casually following the man.

Without so much as glancing at the books and magazines on the first floor, the man began to climb the central staircase that led to the children's section on the second story.

Koumoto Books had always put effort into stocking children's books, and their selection on the second floor rivaled even the collections of their large competitors, something Minami was privately proud of.

However, Emon had also died there.

Some of the visiting customers were interested in seeing the scene of the accident, and they would take it upon themselves to climb to the second floor, then ask Minami and the other workers gruesome questions like *"About where did the owner pass away?"*

Minami had told the other part-timers to politely decline to answer such inquiries, so this man should not have known exactly *where* on the second floor Emon had died. Despite that, he had beelined for the spot and stopped there.

He's…not a shoplifter?

Minami's chest tightened. Her suspicion toward the old man transformed into something much darker and heavier.

Why did he stop right there?
That's where the boss collapsed.

When she had arrived at the shop after the accident, his body had already been removed, and the police had been investigating the scene. But Emon's bloodstain had still remained.

The man was now squinting at the top of the bookshelf, twisting his face as he looked up.

With seeming difficulty and pain, he stretched his neck out and stared intensely; his wrinkled face warped steadily with emotion, and he grew terribly distressed. He looked tense enough to shout something at any second.

The man was staring at the shelf that held the children's dictionaries and illustrated reference books—the very ones that had fallen on Emon's head and taken his life.

Minami's neck stiffened, and a cold sweat broke out on her palms.

Her heart was pounding fast.

The man stood on tiptoe and reached a hand out toward the shelf.

"!"

Minami gasped when she saw the wounds that ran from his palm down to his wrist.

There are so many cuts, it's like he was clawed or bitten—

His wounded hand was heading for the top shelf.

The man was of about average height for his age, maybe 165 or 166 centimeters. His back was slightly bent, but with effort, he stretched up on tiptoe to grasp an illustrated reference book on the top shelf.

Though it was a book for children, it was quite heavy and thick.

He's standing so awkwardly that it could slip out of his hand and hit his head while he's trying to grab it. Then it'll be the boss's accident all over again!

An image of an avalanche of books crashing down on the man flashed through Minami's mind, and her whole body tensed up.

Watch out!

"Sir? If there's a book you need, I'll get it for you."

She called out to him as politely as possible, taking care not to let her suspicion show on her face.

The man's scarred hand trembled, and he turned to face her. Face still racked with tension, he glared at her with sunken eyes.

The intensity of his world-weary gaze made her flinch.

Minami had dealt with many elderly customers. Occasionally, one would start shouting all of a sudden, as if a switch had been flipped, so Minami was on guard now. But she smiled with all her might and asked, "Which book shall I get down?"

The man's shoulders hitched again in surprise, and his dry, cracked lips opened slightly before snapping shut again.

He pulled his injured hand into the sleeve of his coat as if to hide it, his expression hesitant and uneasy, until finally speaking in a hoarse, quiet voice.

"...It's not here."

"Um?"

I don't understand.

He looked like he was reaching out desperately to take a book, though. Is the title he wants not here?

"What sort of book might it be? I'll search for it."

When she asked that, the man's strained, frightened expression collapsed into a look of sorrow. With a frown pulling down the corners of his mouth, he mumbled hopelessly, "...No, it's fine. You won't find it."

"But, sir..."

She was starting to feel dejected, without so much as a guess as to what the man could possibly be searching for.

"I'm sure we have that book here in the store."

Suddenly, someone spoke from behind her.

She turned around in surprise to find Musubu bounding over, his eyes sparkling brightly behind his glasses and his hair fluttering softly as he moved.

Hang on, what did he just say?!

He can't possibly know the title from our exchange just now.

The customer's eyes were also wide open.

Still beaming, Musubu reassured him, "I'll bring it over to you in a moment, so if you would be so kind, please wait here for a bit."

After announcing that clearly, he turned his luminous eyes toward Minami.

"Ms. Tsuburaya, would you help me, please?"

She bowed to the customer as Musubu started walking, then took off after him.

"Hang on, where are you going? What do you mean, help you?"

"Well, I guess I mean that I want your help finding the book the customer wants. I got a hint, but I'm not quite sure what we're looking for."

"What? You don't even know where it is, but you told him you'd bring it to him? You're unbelievable." Feeling as if she might start shouting at any moment, Minami desperately tried to keep her tone in check.

I knew this kid was a weird one! He can't be trusted!

"You turn around right now and go apologize," she insisted.

"Wait a minute, please. I can't possibly do it on my own, but if you work with me, I have a feeling we can find the book, Ms. Tsuburaya."

She had no idea why he was so confident. With a stern expression, she asked, "...What was the hint?"

His face softened with relief, "First, it's something 'big, sharp, and scary.'"

"Huh?" Minami was stunned.

Musubu continued in a flowing tone of voice, "A 'story of long, long, long ago.'"

"Wait a second."

"It's 'not here anymore.'"

"Not here?"

"No, apparently it's in the 'tearoom.'"

"Tearoom...?"

Where is that?

"There's an 'ocean' and 'bird bones,' and it's in a 'blue mausoleum.'"

Minami scowled with her head in her hands, when suddenly she had a realization.

The ocean and bird bones? Could it be?!

Musubu grinned.

"Ah, you've got it?"

She didn't answer; she simply walked off, her lips still pursed.

I thought for sure he was joking around. But bird bones—

She headed straight down an aisle on the second floor all the way to an office at the other end, and she opened the door.

The gray room behind it was about eleven meters square and enclosed by undressed concrete walls. It contained a sofa, a side table, an office desk, and a bookshelf. On the shelf sat miscellaneous books of various sizes and genres.

A single painting of about A4 size hung on the wall across from the bookshelf.

It depicted huge, white bird bones that dominated an ocean beach landscape.

Musubu must have been entering the office for the first time, because when he saw the painting, he mumbled, "So this is where the ocean and bird bones are…" Then he asked Minami, "All right, and the tearoom?"

"…The boss often used to have tea in here, and everyone jokingly called it the Koumoto Café, so…"

The second-floor office was like the boss's second home, and there he would thoughtfully serve all sorts of drinks to suit his guests' tastes, from black tea and coffee to green and herbal tea.

When Minami had first visited the room in middle school, even she'd been served sweet tea by Emon, which she'd drunk with tearful gratitude.

Her throat tightened, and her fingers shook a little; even now, she felt as though she might glimpse a phantom of the man smiling at her from the other side of the steam rising from her cup.

Thankfully, Musubu didn't notice her trembling, as he was examining the wall instead.

"I see—so this must be the 'blue mausoleum,' huh?"

Below the painting was a blue storage chest. He got on his knees, opened it, and dug through the contents. He set many old, beat-up books on the floor beside him before hauling one out with both hands, a sparkle in his eyes.

"Got it!"

Minami had been lost in memories of the past, but when she saw Musubu holding up a book like a piece of treasure, she came back to herself.

"Hang on! Enoki, *that's*—"

"I'm going to go give it to the customer."

"Wait, Enoki!"

By the time she called out to stop him, he had rushed out of the office, book in hand.

She chased after him in a panic.

What do I do? If Enoki gives him a book like that, the customer's probably going to think he's making fun of him and get mad.

Up ahead of her, the anxious Minami could see Musubu handing over the volume to the elderly man with a broad grin, and she could hear his cheerful voice.

*　　*　　*

"My apologies for the wait. I believe this is what you were looking for, sir."

He was holding an illustrated reference book for children. On the cover of the large-format book was the title *The Field Guide of Extinct Animals*, accompanied by images of animals like dinosaurs, a Tasmanian tiger, and a dodo bird.

"Something big, sharp, and scary."

"A story of long, long, long ago."

"Not here anymore."

Sure enough, the book did match the "hints" Musubu had mentioned.

But the reference book in his hands had a stained cover with faded print, and the pages were warped and wavy. A piece of paper with the word *Sample* written on it in red was stuck to the cover, which had been laminated with a clear film.

It was Koumoto Books's policy to put worn and damaged books on the shelf as display samples. The idea was to leave out some titles that were all right to soil, especially in the children's corner, where kids often dirtied them.

The volume Musubu had fished from the blue storage box seemed to have been one such title, but it was quite old and badly damaged all over. It was clear at a glance that it had reached the end of its lifetime even as a display book.

There was no way they could sell such a worn-out, unfit copy to a customer.

She felt a rush of perspiration as she interjected from beside Musubu.

"I'm so sorry, sir—he's new; he only joined our staff the day before yesterday."

She began apologizing.

The man, who had been wearing a pained look until this moment, suddenly opened his sunken eyes wide and stared at the reference book with the *Sample* sticker as if he couldn't believe what he was seeing.

His lips, arms, and shoulders were all trembling.

His expression was not one of anger or disappointment, but rather one filled with deep emotion. Minami fell silent.

A faint pool of tears even welled up in his wrinkle-bound eyes.

His slim, bony, scarred-up hand emerged slowly from the sleeve of his coat, and he extended it to accept the *Field Guide* from Musubu.

As he took the hefty tome, the man's hands jerked downward, and his eyes filled further with tears, as if even the weight itself had an emotional impact.

And then he spoke in a tear-choked voice.

"That's right... I was looking for this. I was certain it had been thrown away long ago, but it was still here..."

The man embraced the book lovingly with hands covered in scars and wrinkles. As Minami watched, the muscles in Musubu's face relaxed, as though a beloved old friend were stroking him like a precious object.

"It's been a long time. Have you been well?"

"You've really grown."

It was almost as if he could hear those words being said aloud. Behind his glasses, his big eyes narrowed joyfully, and his mouth, which still retained some of its childlike innocence, spread into a broad smile.

When the man opened the cover carefully with trembling fingers, he found an image of a tyrannosaurus accompanied by some small writing. Looking down at the illustration, the man's face creased again as he bit his lip and blinked some tears away.

Minami had absolutely no idea what was going on.

But in the seven years she'd worked part-time at Koumoto Books, she had never seen a customer so happy to receive a title she'd located for them—had never seen anyone so joyous.

To this man, that stained, worn-out *Field Guide* was the most important book in the world.

As he blinked and sniffled over and over, he turned the pages with his scarred hands.

"That's right—I wanted to read this book. I wanted to see it again...," he muttered.

Then he told them an old story involving the book.

The old man's name was Michijirou Furukawa, and he was a veterinarian in a neighboring town.

He had received the injuries on his hands from being scratched and bitten by his patients during treatment. Minami was beginning to grasp the situation.

The fraying on his coat, too, was thanks to scratches from the cats he was caring for in his own home. His wife had cautioned him that it looked unbecoming, but he was inclined to be frugal, so he had told her he couldn't throw away something he could still wear.

When Michijirou was still a child, a woman named Natsu Koumoto, the founder of Koumoto Books, had been the proprietor here. Natsu had lost her husband in the war and had started a bookstore in this town while raising her young child.

At the time, the splendid three-story bookstore had been the pride of the town.

From the very first day it opened, everyone had gone there, and it was crowded with people. They said that if you went to Koumoto Books, you could find any sort of book you were looking for.

"My family was poor, you see... There were a lot of us children, and we could never get our parents to buy us luxury items like books. That's why on the way home from school, I would walk one hour to Koumoto Books and stand here reading. It was my greatest joy as a child."

On one of those trips, he had encountered *The Field Guide of Extinct Animals*.

The cover full of illustrations of animals he had never seen before had drawn him in at first glance, and he had read it eagerly from cover to cover. He'd been thrilled by the realistically painted tyrannosaurus, triceratops, dodo, and Tasmanian tiger, and he never tired of gazing at them.

Once he knew about this reference book, going to Koumoto Books became that much more fun. Whether he was sitting in class at school or helping out at home, he thought only of wanting to get back there and read more of it.

The reference book was staggeringly expensive and would have been absolutely out of reach for a family that would have struggled to pay for an ordinary book. Michijirou didn't even get any spending money.

"But I was plenty satisfied simply knowing that it would be there, like a great treasure, if I just went to Koumoto Books."

Even on days when it was drizzling rain or when a cold wind was blowing or when the snow had piled up deep enough to bury his ankles, he still wanted to enjoy the book, so he would hurry down the road to Koumoto Books with red cheeks.

"Ah, I want to read it right now. I want to read!"

And after he would arrive at the usual place and pick up the reference book to begin turning its pages, it was all bliss.

The Tasmanian tiger's fangs were incredibly sharp and strong. Both the triceratops and the tyrannosaurus walked the earth in the distant past, and they left behind gigantic footprints in the ground. Although the dodo had wings, for some reason it just tottered around and couldn't fly.

To Michijirou, it seemed as if the creatures might leap out of the open pages at any second.

It was fun and exciting.

But one day, he realized one of the women working in the shop was watching him. She was tall and thin and wore glasses, with her hair pulled back in a tight ponytail on the back of her head. She always stood up perfectly straight, as if she had a ruler down her back, and her expression was always so stern, as if she was angry, so Michijirou was afraid of her.

That woman was staring right at him.

She must be upset because I've just been standing here reading every day.

Whenever she drew near, his heart pounded, because he knew that one day she would throw him out and tell him to never come back again, that if he wanted the book, he had to bring money and buy it.

He didn't know what he would do if that should happen.

Just thinking about it made his chest tighten and made him feel lonely.

Many children besides Michijirou stood around reading in the children's section, but their parents bought them books when they came to meet them.

Michijirou was probably the only one who had never bought a book, and the sense of inferiority he felt led him to close the reference book and sneak off down the stairs whenever he caught sight of that scary female employee.

Whenever that happened, he would feel miserable and want to cry.

Sometimes an employee in a student uniform would come over to play with the kids in the children's corner. He was really good at reading aloud and was very popular with the children.

Whenever he appeared, they would all shout for his attention.

"Ah, it's Mr. Kanesada!"

"Mr. Kanesada, read this book!"

The children would put books in his hands, and Mr. Kanesada would start reading, skillfully changing his voice to play all the characters, and even the children who were reading on their own would come over to listen.

These were the only times when Michijirou would also stop turning his pages and stealthily incline his ear.

The young man in the school uniform was Kanesada Koumoto, the son of the owner.

One time, when Michijirou had been the only one in the children's section, Kanesada had spoken to him genially.

"Hey, is that interesting?"

He nodded stiffly.

"Great. Well, take your time with it."

He smiled, then left him alone and at ease.

Thus, whenever Kanesada was there, Michijirou felt relieved. Whenever the scary lady was there, however, he felt glum.

"That lady was Kanesada's mother, Natsu, the founder of the store, you know."

The reason why he knew that, he told them, his eyes narrowing with nostalgia as he spoke, was because of what had happened after that—the extremely shocking incident that had followed.

The day that it happened, he'd walked an hour on the way home from school as usual and arrived at Koumoto Books.

Other kids were standing around reading in the children's book corner, and he didn't see any staff nearby.

Thank goodness...

Relieved, Michijirou went over to the usual bookcase and leaned down to pull *The Field Guide of Extinct Animals* off the lowest shelf.

But his beloved *Field Guide* was nowhere to be found.

Huh? Did someone buy it?

His mind went blank.

It was a new publication with an outrageous price tag. The library at his school definitely didn't have it. If someone had purchased the reference book, he would no longer be able to read it at all.

His heart was pounding, and he broke out in a cold sweat.

Could it really have been purchased? Maybe it got put in a different spot by mistake?

Holding his breath, he swept his gaze steadily over the bookcase from top to bottom, then felt another wave of despair creep over him.

"It had been moved to the very top shelf, you see. It was tall enough that it would have been difficult for even an adult to fetch without using a stepladder. For a kid, that was out of the question."

He looked up at his beloved book, which now seemed like a phantom flower blooming at the summit of a mountain, impossible to touch or smell.

He was convinced it had been moved to such a high place so that he couldn't access it anymore, since he had been coming in every day to stand around and read.

With that thought, his eyes grew hot with emotion, and his chest felt as if it would split open with sorrow.

He had no money, and he knew he was in the wrong for only ever reading without buying, so he couldn't say anything to the staff. When he thought about not being able to read the book, Michijirou felt as if all the fun and joy in his daily existence had been ripped out by the roots, as if a gaping, dark hole had suddenly opened up under him.

He was lonesome and heartbroken and miserable, and he knew there was nothing he could do about it.

Tears flooded his eyes, and then someone offered him a book from off to the side.

"You must be looking for this."

Reflected in his blurry field of vision was the reference book he was sure he had lost.

A piece of paper with the word *Sample* in red letters was affixed to the cover.

The person holding it out to him was the scary lady with the stern gaze.

*   *   *

"This copy is for trial reading, so you can read it as much as you like."

The woman's face was the same as always, strict and tense. Her voice was stiff, too.

But when Michijirou was too bewildered to take the book, she pressed it into his arms.

"Here you go.

"When you grow up, come back and buy lots of books, okay?"

With that, she stood up straight and walked away.

Holding the "sample" book in his hands, Michijirou felt like crying again, this time for a completely different reason.

"That's when I realized Natsu was the owner. It also became clear to me that even though she always stood there with a severe look on her face, she was actually watching to make sure all the children in her shop were okay. I'm certain she was concerned about me as well."

Natsu had lost her husband in the war.

During wartime, all amusements had been prohibited. It had been a dark and painful era, when you couldn't even read a book—Natsu, who had wanted nothing more than to read, had decided to open her own bookstore once things were peaceful.

A place where she would be surrounded by so many books that a lifetime wouldn't be enough to read them all; a place the people of her town would get excited to visit because it would have any and every kind of book they might want to read; a place where they could encounter splendid new books, too—that was the kind of store she'd wanted to build.

Still, young Michijirou didn't fully understand all the details about Natsu he overheard from the adults who visited Koumoto Books.

But at the same time, he no longer thought of her as the scary shop lady.

The eyes behind her glasses now looked very earnest, sincere, and beautiful.

Once, he'd asked Natsu what her favorite book was, and she'd informed him that it was the stories her deceased husband had told to her during wartime. Her husband had improvised a tale every night for his wife, who was desperate to read something. To Natsu, her husband, Soratsugu, was a special book all her own. She'd told Michijirou that Kanesada had gotten his skill at reading aloud from Soratsugu.

Her story touched him. He thought this reference book, with *Sample* written on it in big, red letters, was his own special and precious book.

When Michijirou advanced to his third year of middle school, he was old enough to get a job, so he wasn't able to visit Koumoto Books as frequently. Nevertheless, he kept going until he graduated from middle school. Every time he visited, he would take *The Field Guide of Extinct Animals* in his hands and flip through its pages.

It was his special book, after all, the one guaranteed to make him happy.

Someday, I'm going to come buy this book from here.

I'm going to hand over my money to Ms. Natsu, then tell her to please give me this book.

This was what he vowed to himself as he headed to Tokyo to find a job at age fifteen, but daily life in the printing factory where he was first employed proved harsh.

He worked overtime on top of overtime with no breaks and sent almost his entire paycheck back to his family as soon as he got it, with little for himself. Ultimately, his body was broken after five years of work, and the company fired him.

"My dreams and hopes had all been crushed… I came back to this town feeling miserable… And when I visited Koumoto Books for the first time in five years, I felt even worse. I was supposed to save up my money and buy lots of books to pay back the kindness I had received, but Ms. Natsu had already passed away. On top of that, all I had done was accumulate debt, without knowing when I would be able to work again... My future was bleak. I thought I would be better off dying, too, like the extinct animals in the reference book. I felt then that seeing the book might be some comfort."

A broken man, Michijirou had staggered through the shop and climbed the stairs up to the children's book corner, thinking that surely the book wouldn't be there anymore.

"It was."

As he spoke that one phrase packed with a thousand emotions, Michijirou's voice wavered and his eyes watered.

"It had gotten quite damaged since I had last read it five years earlier, and there were even some pages that were torn on the edges. Even so, to see that my precious *Field Guide* was still where I left it was— Well, it set me trembling."

The heat had risen steadily through his throat and eyes, and he'd fought back the rising tears again and again. When he'd found the reference book again, he'd picked it up, blinking repeatedly and shaking slightly. He'd turned the pages.

Recalling the happy boyhood days he'd spent with the book, he'd turned and turned.

"It was almost as if I could hear the book encouraging me, telling me I wasn't extinct just yet. As if it was saying there was still work I could do, that I was just getting started, that I could still give it my all and start anew."

Michijirou's eyes were red, and his voice was filled with passion.

Beside him, Musubu listened with an expression of joy and satisfaction. Every so often, he nodded slightly, as if he was listening to the whisperings of the *Field Guide* that Michijirou was holding with such care.

*   *   *

"You really did your best."

"How admirable. You never gave up, did you?"

"I remember you."

Minami hurried to shake the thought off, chiding herself that it was impossible.

There's no way he can actually hear the voices of books. Even at a time like this, the book can't possibly *be speaking.*

She was mad at herself for even entertaining the idea.

But there was no doubt that *The Field Guide of Extinct Animals* had given Michijirou courage. After he saw the book again, he began working and attending night school and went on to university to become a veterinarian. Now his children were grown, and he was still running his small clinic by himself.

"Neither my son nor my daughter became vets, so the clinic I started will end with me. I'll really be an extinct animal after all… I'll close up shop after my body becomes too weak to work… I've really been feeling my age lately… But I'm glad that I encountered this field guide and that I was able to become who I am today… I've got nothing but appreciation for Koumoto Books. It's hard to believe that not only Kanesada in the second generation, but the third-generation owner, Emon, died so young, too…"

He said that as his life got busy, he'd stopped going out of his way to visit Koumoto Books from the next town over.

When he learned that Emon had died and the store would be closing, he'd felt the same astonishment he'd had as a child when the field guide wasn't in its usual place.

He'd wondered if perhaps the "sample" copy was still there.

A copy of *The Field Guide of Extinct Animals* he'd purchased was already on his bookshelf at home, but that particular display copy was full of happy memories from his childhood. That special book had encouraged him as a young man and helped him to move ahead with his life.

Before Koumoto Books disappeared, he'd wanted more than anything to find out whether that sample copy was still around.

With that single, burning desire, Michijirou had stepped foot into the bookstore he fondly remembered for the first time in more than thirty years.

He'd headed straight for the second story and had been overwhelmed with emotions when he saw that the children's reading corner was still there, same as ever.

The Field Guide of Extinct Animals hadn't been with the other display books or on the shelf, and he'd felt sadness spread over him as he thought, *Of course not…*

He realized that, now that he was an adult, he could probably reach the top shelf, and he had extended a hand toward it.

This was the peculiar movement Minami had witnessed from Michijirou.

Musubu spoke in his cheerful voice. "This book holds a lot of memories, as far as Koumoto Books is concerned, so Emon set it aside. He probably had a hunch that someday someone might come looking for it."

Not even Minami had known that, and she felt her chest tighten at the thought.

She scrunched her lips together to keep herself from asking him how he could possibly have been aware of that.

Deeply moved, Michijirou mumbled, "Is that so…? But how did you know I was searching for this book?"

Musubu smiled sunnily at his puzzled question.

"The books told me, of course!"

Michijirou's eyes opened wide, and Minami grimaced.

"We've got old books on display near the first-floor entrance, right? Valuable books published long ago, signed copies from authors who came to Koumoto Books, that sort of stuff. When you came into the shop, Michijirou, those old books made a real commotion. That's how I knew. I could tell you had a deep connection with this store."

Michijirou seemed as if he didn't entirely understand Musubu's explanation. *Of course not.*

Minami was taken aback at the outlandish story.

But—

"Thank you for visiting our shop today. This book is also happy that it was able to see you, Michijirou. Please feel free to take a photograph with it if you'd like. You could also make a sign!"

When Musubu suggested that, Michijirou held out the reference book in his scarred hands and took a good look at his old friend. Looking at the book as if speaking directly to it, he answered, "I suppose... Since I came all this way, I suppose I'll do that."

When Musubu was done showing Michijirou how the photos and signs worked, he went back down to the first floor and expressed his gratitude to Minami, who had a sullen look on her face.

"Thank you very much for that. I knew from the whisperings of the other books that the one Michijirou was looking for was still in the store, but I couldn't immediately tell where it was based on their explanations. You really helped me out by showing me where to look. Thanks to you, we were able to reunite the book and Michijirou. He was so happy!"

Minami grumbled bluntly, "...Right."

We didn't reunite anyone. We just gave Michijirou a book, *you weirdo.*

Everything Musubu had said just stressed her out.

He kept blabbering on with unclouded eyes, seemingly unaware of Minami's mixed feelings.

"I bet there's been all sorts of drama at Koumoto Books over its many years. With both the purchased books and the ones that remained... I'm sure we'll work to help lots of people meet books here until the very last day. I'm looking forward to it!"

"......"

Musubu considered Michijirou being able to reunite with the book from his memories a real achievement.

This was despite the fact that among the tomes that had rained down on Emon, a new copy of *The Field Guide of Extinct Animals* on the very top shelf had been the one to deliver the fatal blow.

Even Minami understood that she did not need to tell Michijirou that.

But could this harmless, bespectacled high schooler know other things she wasn't aware of?

Surely it had been a coincidence that the book that had sealed the fate of Emon, the owner of the last bookstore in town, had been *The Field Guide of Extinct Animals*, right?

Moreover, the painting of the bird bones that decorated the office where the sample copy had been stashed—its title was *Extinction*.

*"This piece is titled...*Extinction.*"*

The day Minami had first conversed with the owner in that office, he'd smiled gently and told her that.

"It's a lovely painting, isn't it?"

"My father made it. He was the previous owner."

She had stared with calm, clear eyes at the painting of huge bird bones towering over the beach.

It was beautiful and intense—but to Minami, it also looked desolate and a little frightening.

"Who killed Emon?"

She was drawn back to the words Musubu had uttered.

At that moment, he must have heard a response from the volumes lined up on the shelves.

Assuming that books really could talk, they probably would have told him something.

The truth about the boss's death?

With a stiff, tight face, she mumbled, "Hey... Enoki, can you really...?"

Can you really hear the voices of books?

*　　*　　*

She almost asked it aloud.

"Yeah, what's up?" Musubu asked, his tone carefree.

"It's nothing." Minami turned away from him.

She felt her cheeks quickly growing hot, embarrassed to have almost uttered such a stupid question.

There's no way books can talk and no way he can hear them.

Side Story

The
Secret Name
of *Tomb* of
the Wild
Chrysanthemum

The news that Koumoto Books would be closing profoundly impacted Akio.

He'd turned fifty-six this past year and had spent his youth in the small town in Tohoku where Koumoto Books was located.

Standing in the gap between other buildings, the tall and slim bookstore wasn't far from the station and was the first place the townsfolk went when they wanted to buy something to read.

Akio had been a member of the kendo club in high school. As the so-called tough guys of the school, the kendo club members looked down on boys who liked literature as weaklings, would never set foot in a bookstore of their own volition, and didn't even read books unless they had to write a summer book report.

What had turned Koumoto Books into a sacred and bittersweet place for Akio, a special location that set his heart racing, was an unforgettable memory of one Eiko Outake.

In those days, the town had only a girls' high school and a boys' high school, so the genders were naturally separated to study when they reached that point in their education.

There were mixers held with the girls' school all the time, but Akio was a tough guy, so after graduating from middle school, he never spoke to any girl who wasn't in his own family.

However, Akio secretly had eyes for one of the girls from the other school, who always passed by him riding her bicycle along the same route every morning.

He'd never mentioned her to his friends or to anyone else. But the way the wind rustled her hair tied up in a ponytail on top of her head, how the collar of her sailor uniform and hem of her pleated skirt fluttered, and how she pumped the pedals with her feet, clad in white bobby socks and black loafers, left him breathless, with butterflies in his chest and a flush in his cheeks.

Whenever a glimpse of the white nape of her neck or her slim calf leaped into his eyes, he felt guilty, as if he had seen something he shouldn't. Yet at the same time, he also experienced a strange tickle, as if his heart were filling with some sacred emotion.

For some reason, she was the only girl he could recognize even from far away. Akio started heading to school at the right time to coincide with when she would be passing by on her bicycle.

From the gossip of his classmates, he knew that the girl was two years older than him, a third-year high school student named Eiko Outake.

The polished and lovely Eiko was like the Madonna to all the high school boys in the area.

Akio felt nothing but contempt for his classmates who sang Eiko's praises. He considered it disrespectful to join them in their discussions, and he listened to them with a bitter look on his face.

Back then, an older girl seemed utterly unattainable to a boy in high school. He felt like a child compared with Eiko. He couldn't possibly hope to receive any attention from her, much less imagine dating a girl two years his senior.

Simply watching Eiko pass by every morning on her bicycle was a joy for Akio, and he wished for nothing more. Just thinking about anything beyond that would be blasphemy.

That's why he was certain he was delusional when he happened to catch sight of Eiko parking her bike in front of Koumoto Books after school to go inside and found himself entering as well.

Encountering Eiko at a different time and place than usual made him lose his cool and self-restraint in an instant, so he followed her giddily inside.

"Welcome! A student, eh?"

* * *

The man behind the register startled Akio by calling out to him loudly as he entered, nearly causing him to bump into the door with the kendo padding he was carrying on his back.

Since he rarely went into bookstores, he couldn't tell otherwise, but he wondered if the staff was always that energetic.

It sounded just like the exuberant greetings he got from the green-grocer or the fishmonger. The staff member, who looked younger than Akio's father and whom the people in the shop called "boss" or "mister," shouted out cheerfully whenever a customer came in.

"Mr. Yasuda, we got that new Hiroki Itsuki book you've been waiting for! I just love that Natsuko character. It was a touching story. Really moving! I recommend it."

"I tried reading The Inauspicious Skies, *and I got really into it. It's too good at getting you worked up!"*

"Hey, Miyo! Have you read Sazae-San Confidential?*"*

He was greeting everyone like a good friend, and the people he spoke to also seemed to enjoy talking to him about books.

Akio, who was always painstakingly deferential toward the upperclassmen in the rigidly hierarchical kendo club, was rather surprised.

Is this what all liberal arts people are like? Or is this shop owner a special case?

But Akio had more immediate problems. When the owner had greeted him, Eiko, who had entered the shop first, had turned around to look at him. The moment her eyes met his, he froze, stiff as a stone.

I guess now Eiko knows I followed her, huh?

If that were the case, she would certainly be disgusted by him.

What do I do?!

Though his breathing faltered and his back was soaked with sweat, Eiko immediately looked away and walked over to the literature corner without seeming to think anything about him at all.

*   *   *

That's right... Outake has no reason to know who I am.

Even though he had escaped the crisis, that thought disappointed him.

To Eiko, he must have been nothing more than a boy she didn't know from another school who happened to be in the bookstore that day.

She probably wasn't even aware that she had been passing by Akio every day on her way to school as she nimbly pedaled her bicycle.

That's only natural. Fine by me.

Besides, I never had a chance, being two years below her in school and all. I should just be glad I happened to see her and make eye contact today.

On the one hand, it really stung to know that Eiko had never noticed him, but on the other hand, it emboldened him.

What kind of books does Outake read? Let's go take a look.

With that thought, he stealthily followed her to a section of the store.

Eiko was always on her bike when he saw her, so the mere sight of her slender legs as she walked was novel enough to set his heart pounding again.

So svelte...and her hair flows so smoothly. She's so pretty...

She halted. With graceful movements, she picked up one of the slim books stacked on the shelf and slowly began turning its pages.

Akio summoned up all his courage to stand next to Eiko. He, too, pulled a book off the shelf at random, opened it, and pretended to read.

Of course, his attention was entirely focused on the girl standing next to him. Akio couldn't even remember what book he had grabbed.

He had never been in the habit of reading books, so he didn't even know how he would choose one. Right now, anything would do. He simply glided his eyes over the words on the page, not bothering to absorb any of them.

The side of his face in Eiko's direction grew hot. It felt as if he were burning up.

He didn't even turn the pages.

Moving his eyeballs back and forth frantically, he sneaked peeks at Eiko out of the corner of his eye, marveling that the girl who always cycled past him in a flash was right there beside him.

Her pale skin with a light cover of downy hair. Her slim neck. The long eyelashes on her downcast eyes. Her elegant, ladylike nose. Her cherry-colored lips.

His eyes drank it all in, and better yet, the sweet scent of her shampoo drifted over to him, too, making his heart leap. It wasn't just his cheeks and ears anymore that were overheating; now it was his whole head.

His heart was pounding wildly, so fast that he worried about whether Eiko could hear it.

My breathing—am I panting like a wild animal?

Do I stink of sweat, since I came here after practice?

Are my hands and legs trembling badly?

The longer he stood there, the more nervous he became. He wanted to get away from Eiko, but he also wanted to stay there by her side. This dilemma spiraled round and round in his mind until he felt as if he had been spinning in circles on the teacups ride at the amusement park.

It's hard to breathe.

But I'm happy.

Akio's happiness continued until Eiko closed her book, took it to the register, and left the shop.

"Oh! Tomb of the Wild Chrysanthemum, *I see! Good choice. A perfect selection for a high school girl."*

Akio could hear the cheerful voice of the man working the register.

"Tomb of the Wild Chrysanthemum"…?

*   *   *

That was the title of the book Eiko had been reading, and when he glanced down at the stack of books, he saw that they all had the same title.

He returned the book in his hand to the shelf, not having turned a single page, then picked up a copy of *Tomb of the Wild Chrysanthemum* from the pile and carried it to the register without hesitation.

The shopkeeper must have known exactly what was going on after seeing the same book cross the counter twice in a row, and he reacted with a broad grin.

"Ah, well, that's youth!"

Realizing how stupid he was being, Akio felt his face grow hot again.

But he had already brought the book up to the register. He had the man put a cover on it, then took it back, and when his fingers touched the volume, he recalled Eiko's profile and felt a sweet sensation.

By the time Akio left the shop, Eiko was already gone, but his heart was still pounding against the book clutched tight to his chest.

Akio went home and immediately started reading *Tomb of the Wild Chrysanthemum*.

The protagonist, Masao, is in love with his older cousin, Tamiko. She also has feelings for him, so their love is mutual. As the older of the two, Tamiko is bound by family circumstances beyond their control.

To Akio's surprise, Masao was fifteen and Tamiko was seventeen, the same ages as him and Eiko.

It was probably a coincidence, but it immediately aroused his empathy.

The people in their village gossiped about the fact that Tamiko was two years older and had suggested separating the two cousins. Akio's whole body was tense as he read because he understood Masao's emotions all too well.

His heart raced as he mentally overlayed the charms of Tamiko and Eiko.

"I think I must be a reincarnated chrysanthemum flower. Every time I see one, I love it so much I start shaking."

*   *   *

"You like them that much, Tamiko? …No wonder you're like a flower."

"Masao…what about me is like a flower?"

"Well, it's not any specific thing, but somehow you do seem like a chrysanthemum blossom."

"So that's why you like chrysanthemums, Masao…?"

"I love them."

Akio's chest grew unbearably hot as he read their exchange.

He had never gotten so absorbed in reading a book before. This was the first time he'd felt as if a book had been written just for him.

Even after that, Akio never exchanged words with Eiko, and they never made eye contact again. When she would pass him on her bicycle in the mornings on her way to school, he would remember their miraculous meeting at Koumoto Books and watch her go, spellbound.

It had certainly been a moment of joy that day, in that place surrounded by books.

He would never forget that precious memory.

It made his heart leap with delight.

That vibrant, glistening, bittersweet memory.

Eventually, Eiko graduated, and he heard she had gone on to university in Kyoto.

Akio also graduated high school two years later and went to university in Tokyo. He'd stayed in the city, where he'd found a job and gotten married, but his wife had passed away before him.

He didn't have any children, so now, in his midfifties, he was living alone. He had become used to it, and living by himself in the city was pleasant enough.

But sometimes, when he felt lonesome, Akio would reread *Tomb of the Wild Chrysanthemum*.

His marriage to his deceased wife had been arranged by his boss at work, and it had been a loving relationship in its own way.

Nevertheless, he knew there was always a place in the bottom of his heart for the girl he had known once, back in his first year of high school.

"Whenever the last month of the year comes around, I just can't help but think of her. I know we were young at the time, but somehow I can't seem to forget about it."

"More than ten years have passed and it's already ancient history; so many of the details are a blur, but the feelings are as clear as if it happened yesterday. When I recall that time, I'm entirely transported back to what I was feeling then, and my tears won't stop flowing."

"There were both happy and sad times, so I never thought I would forget them. But the more I think of them, the more desperately I crave to return to those dreamlike days."

The opening monologue of the book touched him even more deeply in his fifties than it had in his teens.

Although four decades had passed, the memory of standing next to Eiko in Koumoto Books was still fresh in Akio's mind. He'd assumed that happy place would always be there.

But when he'd spoken on the phone to his parents, who were living with his older brother's family in their hometown, the news of its closing had shaken him.

"Oh yes, the third-generation owner of Koumoto Books passed away. They're going to close up shop. A shame, since it's the last bookstore in town."

Koumoto Books is closing?
The place that held my memory with her is going to disappear?

*   *   *

"Well, you've never been one for reading books, so that's got nothing to do with you, I suppose."

He'd barely heard his mother's words.

When he searched for Koumoto Books online, emotional statements from residents lamenting the closing of the town's last bookstore came up one after another.

He'd found comments from people who had left town as well, expressing their shock that Koumoto Books would be no more. The internet was full of messages from people saying they had always thought it would be there forever.

He discovered that the store would be open for one final week before closing at the end of March.

There were also postings by the shop itself, encouraging people to come during that time and bring their favorite books to take commemorative photographs or to write about their memories associated with those books on colorful paper signs.

Koumoto Books is really going under!

Akio couldn't sit still, so he took leave from work and went home.

His parents and brother had been surprised to hear that he had come back to visit the business before it closed. After all, as his mother had said, Akio had lived a life that had nothing to do with bookstores.

He made some perfunctory excuse to his family, tucked his worn-out, yellowed copy of *Tomb of the Wild Chrysanthemum* into his coat pocket, and set off to visit the store for the first time in over forty years.

It was already the end of March, but compared with Tokyo, winter in Tohoku was long and harsh. He was still cold despite his thick winter coat, and his breath came out white.

Since he'd forgotten how to walk on snowy roads, he slipped and nearly fell down many times along the way.

I've gotten old. This is totally different from back then, when I was in shape and never missed a kendo practice…

Basking in emotional memories, Akio arrived at the slim, three-story bookseller tucked in between buildings on both sides.

Despite the passing of the years, the moment he saw the glass door with the name KOUMOTO BOOKS stenciled on it, he could almost see a vision of the girl in a ponytail parking her bike out front, opening the door, and going inside. Without meaning to, he put his hand over his heart and stood stock-still.

With his heart pounding just as hard as it had back then, he pushed the door open.

"Welcome!"

A boy at the first-floor register was wearing large glasses and an apron, and he cheerfully greeted Akio. His soft-looking black hair bounced lightly when he moved. He looked like a high schooler working part-time.

The way he clearly and brightly informed the customers about the closing sale was reminiscent of the good-humored, jovial second owner.

That man had suddenly taken ill and had passed away young.

And now his son, who had inherited the shop after him, had lost his life to an unfortunate accident.

The last bookstore in town would soon be closing up shop.

Near the entrance, rare titles and books signed by visiting authors were on display.

One that stood out among them was *A Funeral for Kanoyama Books*, a bestseller from about twenty years ago that had been so popular that even Akio, who didn't read books, knew its title and basic story. The author, Kouichi Tamogami, was from this town, and there was even a signed copy in his parents' house.

Such a famous guy held a signing in a place like this, huh...?

I guess books were really booming back then...

It had been an era when everyone was reading and talking about books, and bookstores had a real sheen to them.

The same was true of Akio.

It had been a youthful time, when his heart had danced and his cheeks had flushed, and he'd felt love bubbling up inside himself.

Back then, he had been really inexperienced and awkward.

If I had been who I am now, I bet I could have acted a little slicker around Eiko…

Akio had heard that, after graduating from university, she had gotten married in Kyoto.

So maybe—

But that was nothing more than a pointless daydream.

He smiled bitterly at himself for fantasizing as the boy in glasses explained how to write a paper sign for the store's closing sale.

"Did you bring a book with you today?" the boy asked.

Feeling awkward, Akio pulled *Tomb of the Wild Chrysanthemum* from his pocket.

"It's not a book for an old guy like me, but I was young once, too, forty years ago."

Behind his glasses, the boy's eyes widened slightly.

With an expression as if he was straining his ears to hear something, he stared at the image of a chrysanthemum on the cover.

What's going on?

He wondered if the boy was surprised to see that a man in his fifties had been holding on dearly to *Tomb of the Wild Chrysanthemum*.

As Akio stood there, regretting showing anyone his book, the boy's big eyes suddenly shifted and looked up at him, sparkling behind his lenses.

"Sir, by any chance, were you in the kendo club?"

"Huh? Uh, yeah…in high school."

Why would he ask something like that? And how did he know I was in the kendo club?

With an even more cheerful expression than before, the boy shouted happily, "I knew it! Sir, thank you so much for reading this book over and over until it got this worn out! The book is very happy about it."

The boy bowed deeply to him as he said these words of thanks, as if he was a friend of the book itself.

"I'm certain this is the book's way of returning the favor. There's someone here who has been waiting for you. Please come with me."

As he came out from behind the register, the boy seemed impassioned, as if he might run off at any second. Akio was dumbfounded.

What the…? What on earth is happening?

"Wait, Enoki!"

Startled, the other staff member who had been behind the register shouted after him.

"Sorry, Ms. Tsuburaya! The book is saying this can't wait! I'll be right back!"

With a smile of boundless cheer on his face, the boy answered the clever-looking woman whom he had called Tsuburaya.

Still bewildered, Akio quickened his pace at the boy's urging.

Someone waiting?

A book returning a favor?

I don't get it at all. What's this kid talking about?

"Hey, kid, who the heck—"

—are you? He didn't get to finish his question, because just then the boy turned around, and with happiness glistening in his eyes behind his glasses, he said—

"I am a voice for books!"

Akio was even more confused than before, and the small, bespectacled clerk hurried on ahead impatiently, his black hair bouncing softly and the hem of his store apron fluttering. He went straight down the aisle to the literature section on the first floor, then turned and turned again.

He was headed for the paperbacks area, where a desk had been set up for people to create their paper signs.

Right in front of them was a slim woman bent over the table, writing on her sign. The moment Akio saw her, his heart nearly stopped.

Forty-one years had passed, but he knew her at a glance.

She had kept her looks—her downturned eyes, her graceful neck, her elegant nose and mouth.

And even now, after more than forty years, she still projected an elegance like a blossoming flower.

Eiko Outake! The girl on the bike!

*　　*　　*

He tightened his grip on the copy of *Tomb of the Wild Chrysanthemum* in his hand.

The employee with the glasses called out to the woman in a sunny voice. *"Ms. Outake!"*

Eiko lifted her head and looked at Akio.

Their eyes met, just as they had years earlier.

Back then, Eiko had quickly averted her eyes, but this time she kept them on Akio's face and opened them wide.

She put one pale hand to her mouth and made an expression as if she couldn't believe what was happening.

In Akio's hand was his battered and yellowed paperback copy of *Tomb of the Wild Chrysanthemum*.

When Eiko saw it, her eyes opened even wider in surprise, and she bit her lip hard, as if trying to keep her emotions from overflowing. She grabbed a book that was sitting on the table and turned the cover toward Akio.

That's Tomb of the Wild Chrysanthemum*!*

It was the same book as the one Akio was holding, in the same size, with the same cover, and it was equally beat-up and yellowed.

As if a strong force drew the copy of *Tomb of the Wild Chrysanthemum* in Akio's hand to the copy Eiko was holding, he walked right past the boy in the glasses as if in a trance until he was face-to-face with Eiko.

She approached him in the same way.

And then, for the first time ever—

—fifty-six-year-old Akio and fifty-eight-year-old Eiko stood opposite each other and exchanged words.

"So those two have been in love with each other this whole time, huh?"

Minami had chased after Musubu, and now she was watching in amazement as the pair in their fifties stood in front of the table in the literature corner, conversing awkwardly. Musubu had filled her in after she'd arrived, and she'd been even more surprised.

About thirty minutes earlier, a beautiful woman had come into the shop carrying a copy of *Tomb of the Wild Chrysanthemum*, and when Musubu had pried for more information about it, Minami had overheard her bashful answer.

"This book is a memento of someone I liked when I was in high school.

"I passed him frequently in the mornings on my way to school, though I was on my bicycle. He was in the kendo club and always carried a bag with his pads in it on his back. That made him look very manly, and my heart would start pounding every time I passed him.

"His name and class were written on his kendo bag, so I knew he was two years younger than me, and I tried desperately to make sure he never became aware of my feelings. Back then, things were different, and I couldn't have casually dated a boy two years my junior, you see."

She'd spoken happily about the one and only time she'd happened to see him in Koumoto Books.

The boy had followed her right after she'd entered the store and had stood next to her for a long time reading a book.

"That day, I actually came in to buy some manga on the third floor, but once I knew he had seen me, I tried to show off. I walked over to the literature corner, a section I normally never went to, and the book I happened to pick up was this one, Tomb of the Wild Chrysanthemum.

"Just like us, Tamiko was two years older than Masao. I knew the plot already, but that was the first time I had ever read it properly… The exchanges between the characters made me feel bittersweet.

"I read it over and over again, and I always felt sad at the ending and cried.

*   *   *

"If Tamiko had been the same age as Masao, they might have gotten married..."

The woman had once been married, but they had never been able to have children and had divorced ten years ago. Now she operated a nail salon in Tokyo.

Even now, she sometimes reread *Tomb of the Wild Chrysanthemum* and recalled the sweet and wonderful thing that had taken place at Koumoto Books, setting her heart aflutter.

"I'm sure that boy got married long ago and probably has children, too. But we're all free to imagine, after all."

She had smiled gracefully as she said that.

Musubu seemed amused when he told the pair, "Come to think of it, it's interesting that the book Eiko has goes by 'Masao,' while the book Akio has is 'Tamiko.'"

She had "Masao."

He had "Tamiko."

Each one of them had taken great care of the book they owned.

"Even among books with the same title, each copy has its own gender and a different personality. In your case, the feelings you had for one another probably influenced your books, pushing them toward one role or the other. That's why I'm sure it was inevitable that the two of you would meet again here at Koumoto Books," he asserted with a bright smile.

Books have personalities, and he can hear their voices? I knew there was something weird about this guy.

Minami was getting irritated at how Musubu was speaking as if this all somehow made perfect sense.

But the thought of two people who bought the same titles at Koumoto Books being tied together does make me happy...

The books pulling toward and calling out for each other.
It would be nice if it were true.

"I think books have a power to bind people together."

Emon had frequently told that to Minami in his calm, gentle voice as he poured tea in the gray office that smelled of flowers.

"People who read the same books empathize with each other and become closer. The books become a starting point for conversation... One person gives a book that is special and important to them to another...

"People can make real connections through books like that. I think it's wonderful to be able to help that happen."

I'm sure the boss would be smiling if he were here now...
"I heard Tamiko and Masao calling out bravely to each other over and over again, and my heart was touched. Old romance novels are so naive and adorable, aren't they?"
Musubu's eyes narrowed happily behind his lenses, almost as if he himself had been linked to somebody by love.
He looks a little like the boss when he does that...

"I am a voice for books."

Minami had also heard Musubu jovially make this declaration—his tone and words, so much like something Emon would have said, had caused her chest to tighten...
Suddenly, Musubu started up again.
"Huh! No, you're wrong—I'm not cheating, Princess Yonaga!"
From his apron pocket, he frantically produced a slim volume with a blue cover and started making excuses.
"It's true! I just thought it was kind of cute, that's all, but not in like a 'love' kind of way— Come on, you're exactly my type, and you know it.

An oleander flower excites me way more than a simple chrysanthemum or bellflower— No, I don't mean to say that you're a poisonous flower, Princess— I love you, all right, so stop cursing me!"

Minami stood beside him, grimacing.

Ah, I really can't stand this guy.

I don't get how someone can actually believe he's capable of talking with books, much less dating them.

Still, Musubu looked funny darting his eyes around and breaking out into a sweat as he groveled to his "girlfriend." Ever so slightly—just a tiny bit, really—Minami smiled.

Book
2

The
Pride of
The Seagull

It had been autumn almost twenty years ago when Asuka had waited in line for a book signing by a bestselling author who was visiting Koumoto Books.

At the time, she had been in her second year of high school. Even now, she still remembered being so excited that it was as if she were walking on air when she heard about the triumphant return of Kouichi Tamogami after he had achieved great success in the city.

Back then, Asuka had wanted to be an actress.

At her high school in this small Tohoku town, the best she could do was join the theater club, but she dreamed of going to Tokyo after graduation and putting her all into auditions so she could become a famous actress.

Her most charming features were her big, bright eyes and her plump lips. When she was in middle school, high school boys would often hit on her. By the time she was in high school, she was getting overtures from college students and adults, but Asuka never dated any of them.

She was young, beautiful, and talented, and she knew her value.

So she didn't want to sell herself short by hooking up with the type of guy who was going to waste away in a tiny town like this one.

She was going to land an exceptional guy who had status, money, and influence and use him as a foothold to become a sparkling actress on the center of the stage.

Asuka had thought this in all seriousness, and she'd believed she could achieve her dreams.

To lose the accent characteristic of her hometown, Asuka imitated how young talent spoke on TV. She diligently cared for her skin and hair, and she took dance lessons to maintain her figure and stamina.

That's why she figured her chance had arrived when she heard that Kouichi Tamogami would be holding a book signing at Koumoto Books. No need to wait for graduation.

Although Mr. Tamogami was thirteen years older than Asuka, he was, judging by his interview photos, a deeply handsome man with chiseled features and an eye for dressing stylishly. He had all the confidence and sex appeal of a man of status.

Once, he had worked as a public servant in his hometown, but at age twenty-eight, the manuscript he'd submitted to a competition won the publishing company's prize for new writers and had become his debut novel.

A Funeral for Kanoyama Books told the story of the closing of the sole bookstore in a snowy rural town. It was funny and warm, a "tearjerker" of a tale about the various customers who visited the store on its final day.

It became an instant bestseller, and a hit movie adaptation with a long cast list of famous actors and actresses soon followed. It was slated to become a new television drama as well. At the moment, Mr. Tamogami was the biggest author around.

His good looks and conversational skills led to frequent appearances in the media, so Asuka was certain he must have had connections and influence.

If Mr. Tamogami took a liking to her, then she might have been able to get him to recommend her for a role when it came time to transpose his novel into a new medium.

With this rose-colored future running restlessly through her mind, Asuka spent three hours on her preparations the day of the signing.

She started by carefully washing her hair and body in the bath, then applied natural-looking makeup, styled her hair to cascade smoothly over her shoulders, and lastly donned her high school uniform.

It wasn't stylish like those worn by the girls in the city. Rather, it was an ordinary and unsophisticated sailor uniform, but there was no better outfit to emphasize her youth.

Heart pounding with nervousness, she walked over to the narrow three-story building not far from the train station, only to find that a line had formed outside the shop.

I'm late!

Asuka had underestimated Mr. Tamogami's popularity.

Flustered, she purchased his new book at the first-floor register, then got in line.

She had purposely chosen to buy his latest title instead of his big hit because she calculated she would have more appeal if she seemed different from all the other bandwagon fans.

Asuka figured he must be tired of hearing everyone's reviews of *A Funeral for Kanoyama Books* and would find that boring. As an author, he would certainly be happier to hear someone say they had bought and enjoyed his latest work.

If she felt like it, she could even try saying something like *your debut novel was also really great, but I thought your new story was more moving.*

Everyone else in line was holding a copy of *A Funeral for Kanoyama Books*, and Asuka felt a little bit proud of herself.

See? I knew it.

I'm different from all you people.

With her heart full of anticipation, she waited almost two hours.

While she was in line, the owner, a kindly-looking man in glasses, came out of the shop with a sweet and welcoming lady who seemed to be his wife. They distributed drinks in paper cups and pieces of chocolate to those in the queue.

"Thank you for visiting our shop today. Our apologies for the delay. If you'd like, you could pass the time by reading Mr. Tamogami's books. They're quite entertaining, so your wait will go by in a flash."

The shop owner looked on with gentle eyes from behind his glasses as he spoke. Beside him, his beaming wife held out a basket filled with individually wrapped chocolates.

Eventually, finally, Asuka stood before Kouichi Tamogami.

He looks just like the photos I saw in the articles!

That should have been obvious, since he was the man himself, but her heart pounded at the sight of him.

Kouichi Tamogami in the flesh was also a handsome man with chiseled features. He wore a suit that appeared to be from an Italian brand, and he was overflowing with confidence and sex appeal.

This is what someone who fled this little town to find success in the big city looks like.

Asuka felt as if her entire body had become one big heart, the throbbing intensifying.

She held out her book.

"Oh, the new one!"

Mr. Tamogami's eyes opened a little wider, and his expression softened. When she saw that, Asuka was glad she had chosen his new book.

A hint of interest in his eyes, he raised his head to gaze at Asuka. A look of appreciation passed over his face as he took in Asuka's youth and beauty, and his manly, sensual mouth spread into an even wider smile.

"You're a high school student? What year?"

"I'm in my second year, seventeen years old."

She made sure to smile not as if she was flirting but rather to give off a sense of innocence and bashfulness.

But not too timid, still cheerful.

The night before, she had practiced thoroughly in front of a mirror, so she was sure she must be smiling the way she intended.

She could tell it was working from Mr. Tamogami's reaction, the way he narrowed his eyes as though looking at something radiant.

*   *   *

"Seventeen, huh? So young..."

"You're young yourself—er, I mean...you look even cooler in person."

"Ah-ha-ha, I can't believe I'm getting compliments from a high school girl. Thank you. I'm glad I held this book signing. This new novel might be a little difficult for someone your age, but please give it a read."

"Okay! Um...after I read it, could I send you my thoughts?"

"Of course. I'm already looking forward to it... Ah, so your name is Asuka. Like the Asuka period of Japanese history. That's a great name."

Asuka had taken out the piece of paper where she'd written down the name she wanted him to mention when he signed the book. Mr. Tamogami had looked at the paper and had commented on it.

"Thank you very much. I like that the characters can also mean a 'bird in flight.' So I'm happy you had the same thought."

That part was true.

When she was in elementary school, Asuka had hated being the only one with her name written in katakana, so she had come up with some kanji characters for it. She'd thought that being a "bird in flight" was cool, so that's how she'd decided to think about her name.

Whenever she told someone her name or wrote it down, she always thought of herself as a "bird in flight" on the inside.

I've never told anyone that, but...

That was the moment that made Asuka's heart truly start pounding, not out of any self-interested calculations. She smiled broadly with her whole face. She had been thoroughly charmed.

Tamogami's expression changed again slightly when he saw her smile. He looked surprised, then just a little hurt for some reason.

But that expression soon faded as he ran his signing pen across the inside of the front cover with a practiced hand.

To Asuka Kanno

From Kouichi Tamogami

He wrote her name using kanji, and Asuka's cheeks grew even hotter.

"Thank you so much! I'll treasure it!"

Clutching the book tightly to her chest, she thanked him and left.

She knew she'd stirred something in him.

So Asuka decided to make another attempt.

After the book signing had ended, she'd waited for Mr. Tamogami to come out the back door of the bookstore.

She hung around the exit like a devoted fan.

Some famous people don't like that, and in those cases, it can have the opposite effect from what's intended and give a bad impression.

However, Asuka thought there was a good chance of success from the sense of Mr. Tamogami she'd gotten during the signing. She could tell he was interested by the way he'd looked at her.

Though it was still autumn, the temperature dropped steadily as the sun went down, and she grew cold because she was only in her sailor uniform.

He just wasn't coming out. She wondered if he'd already gone home.

By the time the door opened and Mr. Tamogami stepped out wearing a trench coat, Asuka was hugging her shoulders with frigid hands and sniffling dejectedly.

He was speaking to that kind-looking owner with the glasses from the doorway.

*   *   *

"Kouichi, thank you so much for today. All the customers were so pleased. Come again sometime."

"…Sure, it was fun for me, too, Emon… And Yaeko…she looks well; that's a relief."

"You should stay a while longer next time. My wife wants to treat you to some of her home cooking. And if you're so inclined, I'd like to take you up to my office and spend all night chatting like we used to."

"…We're not young anymore, so I don't know about that… But I'll look forward to Yaeko's cooking."

"All right, I'll tell her. Tamogami…talk to you later, yeah?"

"I don't really answer my phone when I get busy writing, so if you could send an e-mail or fax, that would be great."

"Got it. I'll e-mail you."

Tamogami said good-bye with a smile, turned his back on the bookstore owner, and walked off. The owner waved as he left, his eyes narrowed in a gentle grin.

Asuka followed after the author.

I've got to say something to him before he gets to the station.

Once we get past this road, there will be lots more people.

It's now or never.

"Mr. Tamogami!"

When she saw what he looked like when he turned around, Asuka felt as if she had been doused in ice water and was instantly regretful.

For whatever reason, he wore an incredibly grim expression.

His face was twisted in pain, and he was clenching his teeth.

Intense anger and anguish filled his eyes, and he glared at her as if seeking somewhere to discharge those emotions.

He looks like a totally different person than at the signing!

Tamogami looked as though he had just committed murder a moment ago. That's how fierce and violent he appeared.

Is this man really the same Tamogami I met this afternoon?

"Uh, um…I… Your new book, I…started reading it, and I enjoyed it… I couldn't put it down…and I really wanted to give you my thoughts…right away…so I…"

Both Asuka's voice and legs were trembling.

He's scary!

I want to run away!

She knew her face must have been pitiful, like a stupid baby rabbit that had happened upon a wolf.

Tamogami seemed to realize she was the high school student who had come to his book signing, and the blazing light disappeared from his eyes.

But in its place, exhaustion and distress marred his face as he questioned her.

"Oh…it's you. Did you wait for me this whole time? Weren't you cold?"

"N-no. I'm fine. Besides, I was reading your book as I waited, so the time flew by."

Tamogami grimaced at the phrase Asuka had borrowed from the bespectacled shop owner. Then he put on a weak smile, stretched out his hand, and touched Asuka's cheek.

At that moment, she felt as if his large hand could crush her whole face, and a chill went up her spine.

                     *   *   *

"Ah, I knew you'd be cold."

His warm palm completely covered Asuka's right cheek.
His dark eyes glared down at her.
Scared.
I'm scared.

"I'm...fine."

She just barely managed to mumble the words.
When she did, Tamogami responded in a mild voice this time, with an extremely tender look in his eye.

"You're like Nina from The Seagull.*"*

"Seagull...?"

"It's a play by Chekhov. Nina's the heroine. She dreams of becoming an actress."

An actress!
Her heart had been calmed by Tamogami's gentle tone of voice, but now it began pounding again.
It was as if he'd pierced straight through to the motivation behind Asuka's actions.
This was probably not his first encounter with a girl who was trying to get close to a famous and influential person—just as Asuka was.
I'm sure that's what happened.
I'm such an idiot!
He must hate me for being a selfish, wanton girl.

"If you're Nina, that must make me Trigorin, the author who takes her away with him to the city."

*   *   *

He had figured out everything, including that Asuka longed to escape to the city, far away from this small town.

But there was no backing out now.

She didn't know what kind of person Trigorin was or what happened to Nina.

But—

"So what will you do? I'll probably ruin you, you know."

A dark shadow had again descended over Tamogami's face as he looked down at Asuka. The smile had completely disappeared from his lips, and some kind of heartrending emotion was welling up in his narrowed eyes.

Why is this man making such a miserable face? He looks like he can see my future and feels sorry for me.

Summoning all her courage, Asuka answered him.

"That's fine."

◇   ◇   ◇

"…Almost twenty years have gone by since then."

Now thirty-six, Asuka mumbled this as she stared vacantly at the snow-covered rice paddies and fields that flowed past the train window.

She had spent one night with Tamogami when she was seventeen, then dropped out of high school at eighteen and started living with him in his Tokyo apartment.

That had lasted only three years.

No, better to say they'd kept it going for three whole years.

Tamogami could have cast her aside after a single night, so in some sense their relationship had been quite serious.

Through his intervention, Asuka had been able to attach herself to an entertainment company and had performed small parts in television dramas and onstage.

After she'd separated from Tamogami, she'd quit the company and had become a free agent, and now she was an actress with a small theatrical troupe.

They didn't perform in public exhibitions or at big fancy theaters. No, their shows were in underground venues where the audience sat on plastic sheets while they watched.

Of course, that didn't pay enough to live on, so she worked in a night-club as well, but considering her age, she wasn't sure how long she could keep doing that.

Asuka's value had dropped substantially.

"Just like Nina in *The Seagull*, huh…?"

Even now, she frequently reread her small copy of Chekhov's collected plays.

The aspiring actress Nina falls in love with Trigorin, a much-older writer of about her father's age who visits her village, and she goes to the city with him.

However, she never gets ahold of the success she dreams of, and Trigorin reconciles with a lover from his past.

Nina just barely continues to scrape by as an actress, sometimes stealthily returning to her home village to look at the handmade stage where she had stood as a young girl.

Nina's situation was just like the one Asuka found herself in now.

Asuka had first met Tamogami at Koumoto Books. When she'd learned that it was closing, she'd gotten the urge to see the place that held so many feelings one last time before it disappeared, no matter what. She'd packed her paperback copy of *The Seagull*, which included the namesake work and other Chekhov plays, plus the barest essentials in a small suitcase, and had gotten on the train.

She could have saved money by not taking the Shinkansen, but that would have cost time. The high-speed train could get her there in lit-tle over an hour—otherwise, it was a four-hour trip that included train changes and waiting times.

As she stared vacantly out the window, she recalled this and that from the past and felt herself getting choked up. The passing scenery grew wintrier along the way, and as the temperature dropped, the number of riders decreased, until eventually Asuka was the only person in the car.

In a hoarse voice, she mumbled some of Nina's lines, which she had entirely memorized.

"'To know the joy of becoming a writer or actress, I would be hated, or impoverished, or disillusioned, and endure it all gladly.

"'I would live in an attic, and eat nothing but brown bread, and I would not let dissatisfaction with myself or awareness of my own immaturity trouble me.

"'In exchange, I would demand fame…real fame, the kind that brings the house down.'"

After she had separated from Tamogami, these were the lines she had frequently recited to herself when she was living in a small one-room apartment in a thirty-year-old building on the edge of the city.

I just have to get through this.
I'll be fine. I'm still young.
I'm only twenty-one.
I'm going to make a name for myself—this is only the beginning.

I wonder how I was able to be so hopeful…

It really seemed like I was special, like I was one of the chosen ones…

At thirty-six, Asuka was still languishing as an undiscovered actress.

As the world outside the train window turned a gloomy gray, her heart gradually became dark and depressed.

Those snow-covered mountains and fields, so unlike the city she was used to—instead of making her feel nostalgic, the sight made Asuka's chest tighten.

She felt as if she were trapped inside the cold, heavy snow, with her limbs going stiff, freezing solid.

Whenever the train stopped and the doors opened, a sharp chill blew in.

A group of girls in high school uniforms appeared with the cold wind. It must have been time for them to return home from school. The quiet interior of the train car suddenly became lively, and Asuka breathed a sigh of relief.

As long as she was alone, she would have sunk deeper and deeper into her feelings.

She didn't mind the voices of others.

She felt peace of mind in the middle of a crowd.

The girls seemed to be having fun, chatting about their club activities and their crushes. They gently elongated the ends of their words in a way the girls in Tokyo didn't, in the characteristic accent of the region.

Ah…I'm home.

When she had been a student, everyone around Asuka had spoken like that, even as she'd tried her best not to.

But when she'd joined the entertainment company in Tokyo, it had been the first thing they told her.

"You've got an accent. You'd better fix it. Or would you rather play provincial characters? If you go that route, your roles will be limited, and you'll do best on variety shows."

That had been a shock, since she had always thought she had no accent, unlike the other girls in her town.

She had long since lost the accent.

But here in this train car, the fact that only she could speak in the standard dialect didn't feel like something special. It felt lonely.

I don't belong to this place anymore.

On the few occasions she'd returned to visit her hometown, she had felt strange and out of place, and even though she'd never had anything waiting for her back in Tokyo, she'd nevertheless always been eager to return.

After repeating that experience several times, she'd stopped visiting altogether.

She wasn't even sure when she'd last been home.

…Oh yeah. It was after the earthquake.

Almost ten years earlier.

When Asuka had been twenty-six, a huge earthquake had occurred in Tohoku.

Asuka had been glued to the news in her Tokyo apartment, on the flat-screen LCD TV she'd just purchased. With a stiff face and held breath, she had watched buildings collapse and the black tsunami waters swallow everything up, unable to believe what she'd been seeing.

There had been little damage to Asuka's hometown, and even electricity and gas had been restored quickly.

Nonetheless, when she returned home the day after the earthquake, Asuka was met with recurring views of cracked walls, collapsed fences, and piles of rubble. The effects of the earthquake were everywhere; she felt her chest constrict sharply, and she started to hyperventilate at the sight.

The main street of town was lined with closed and shuttered businesses. It seemed as if the town was headed for extinction, and that frightened her.

Even after she'd gone back to Tokyo, the news she'd received from home had been all about some store closing or some school being shut down, and she would get choked up every time.

At last, the train arrived at her home station.

She headed straight for Koumoto Books, before even getting on the bus to her parents' house.

The store was about a three-minute walk from the station but in the opposite direction from the main street. Despite that, the area had gotten a fair amount of foot traffic and had usually been crowded with people when Asuka had been a high schooler. Now it was deserted.

I know it's a weekday evening, but… there aren't many people around, and the stores don't have any life to them, just as I feared.

It seemed as if the whole street was in a slow decline.

I wonder if the main street over there is in the same state...

If that were the case, then Asuka's hometown was disappearing for sure.

The closing of Koumoto Books seemed like a symbol of the downturn.

After the earthquake, the five bookstores in town had closed one after the other, and Koumoto Books lived on as the only one left.

Its continued existence had been a source of stability for Asuka.

A reminder of how her seventeen-year-old self had believed so proudly in her own future and been so full of glittering dreams.

That place where Tamogami had given her the compliment *"Ah, so your name is Asuka. Like the Asuka period of Japanese history. That's a great name"* at the book signing and her heart had fluttered—where he had squinted in the brilliance of her youth and beauty.

She had been comforted by its existence.

It's disappearing.

She walked down the snow-covered street feeling irritated.

There was no need for snow boots in Tokyo, so she didn't have any. She could barely keep her footing in her sneakers.

In high school, commuting on her bicycle down the roads frozen over by snow had been no trouble at all, but now she found that just walking posed a daunting challenge. What should have been a mere three-minute stroll from the station felt interminably long, and when she finally arrived in front of the door that said KOUMOTO BOOKS, she was incredibly relieved to find that the narrow three-story building was still there.

Hard to believe it's really going to close in four days...

Just as she extended a hand to open the door, she stopped at the thought that Tamogami might be inside.

He had a connection to Koumoto Books, both as the place where he had held a book signing and as the last bookstore in his hometown.

Plus, the idea for a grand store closing where people brought their favorite books and made colorful signs was obviously based on Tamogami's most famous work, *A Funeral for Kanoyama Books*.

And that wasn't all. Tamogami had been close friends with the owner who had passed away, and the two were nearly the same age.

He'd called the quiet, kindly man with the glasses "Emon."

Emon's wife had given birth while Asuka was living with Tamogami, so she had gone with him to buy them a present.

When they were picking out baby clothes in a department store, Tamogami had been wearing a dreary expression and been acting strangely.

He'd also spoken in a kind of evasive way when later he'd received a thank-you call from Emon, and he'd had a deathly grim look in his eyes after he hung up.

When Asuka had said, *"I want to see Emon's baby,"* his voice and body had both stiffened as he'd answered that he had too many deadlines to make the trip.

It had been obvious that something had probably transpired between him and Emon.

Even so, there was no mistaking the fact that Koumoto Books and its owner were very important to Tamogami. When he was drunk or had his guard down, he would tell stories of the old days with a pained expression.

He spoke about how Emon's wife, Yaeko, would bring them meals while chiding them that they could just as easily talk in the house.

"There was a painting...mounted on the office wall. It depicted some huge bird bones that had been discarded on a beach... Apparently, the artist was Emon's dad.

"His name was Kanesada...a cheerful, handsome guy who had a knack for painting. He was also skilled at reading aloud to others, and Emon always said that if he hadn't worked in the bookstore, he probably would have become a painter or an actor...

"He died young from illness, so he probably titled that painting Extinction *because he himself had a hunch about what was coming... I wonder, is that painting...is it still in that same spot in that room...?"*

*   *   *

As he spoke in a voice filled with yearning, his expression would gradually grow gloomier. At such times, he would grumble out dispassionately some lines from *The Seagull*...

"'Men, and lions, and eagles, and quails...

"'...all living things, all creatures great and small, having finished their dreary rounds, have disappeared.

"'After many thousands of centuries, the earth carries not one living thing. Only the miserable moon continues shining its light in vain.'"

In a low voice, sadly, so sadly...
Tears would trickle down his cheeks.
Asuka lived with him for three years, but he never let her know what he was hiding inside.
He never told her what he wanted.
He never told her why he took her in.
He never even told her if he loved her.
Tamogami never let her see his true feelings, and when she grew tired of trying to guess, she left.
Despite that, he still had a strong pull on her.
Even after they'd separated, she'd kept thinking about his feelings.
He was still a total enigma—but she had sensed that he was simultaneously avoiding Koumoto Books and Emon, while also longing to visit.
So Tamogami is probably...here.
There's a good chance I'll see him again.

*But...*I knew that before I came here, *didn't I?*

Asuka laughed at herself for worrying about that now.
After all, when she had heard that Koumoto Books would be open for

one last week before closing, the first thing that had popped up in her mind had been that she might find Tamogami there.

I want to see him.

But now that I'm thirty-six and not seventeen, I won't be able to charm him again.
Just the possibility he would think that I've grown dull and ugly with age repulses me.
I don't want to see him.

Asuka was of two minds about it, and she stood there for a long time, warring with herself.
I want to see him.
I'm afraid to see him. I don't want to.

What will happen if I see him now?
Tamogami couldn't change Asuka's unhappy life, nor did she want him to.
For one thing, his influence as a writer had waned since then.
So why can't I help but want to see him?

Another customer came up behind her. Asuka was standing in front of the entrance, blocking the way. She pushed forcefully against the door and stepped into the shop.
"Welcome!"
A boy in glasses behind the first-floor register greeted her cheerfully. His soft-looking black hair bounced a little as he moved.
"Did you bring a book with you today, ma'am? We're doing photographs and making displays over there, so please feel free to participate."
After briskly informing her of this in a pleasant voice, he suddenly made a strange face.

"Huh?"

*   *   *

He blinked in surprise behind his glasses and looked as if he was straining his ears to hear something. Several seconds passed—and finally, he smiled and spoke again.

"Excuse me, but *I feel as if I've met you somewhere before.* Have you been on television, by any chance?"

"…No."

Asuka answered with a bitter smile.

Even if he had seen some program she had appeared in, she was probably in either a background role or, at best, the part of a wife forced into sex work by her husband's secret debts in some awful reenactment clip.

She was embarrassed to be thought of as an actress who could only get those types of roles.

"Is that so? You're so lovely, I thought for sure that was it. Please excuse me."

His carefree way of talking resembled that of the late owner a little. Emon had also worn glasses and had had a gentle, kind face, too. If someone had told her he was Emon's kid, she probably would have believed them.

As she walked away from the register, she heard the boy with glasses quietly making excuses to somebody.

"Wah, it's not cheating! I just said that because *everyone was making a fuss.* Anyway, it wasn't cheating."

The boy's girlfriend had probably come to hang out at the shop and had gotten jealous from overhearing his exchange with Asuka a moment ago.

Somehow that seemed sweet and left her with a bit of a tender feeling.

Come to think of it, that boy with glasses didn't have an accent…

Did he come here from somewhere else?

She didn't have long to think about it.

When Asuka discovered there was a copy of *The Seagull* on a shelf in the paperbacks corner, a copy that had the exact same cover as the book she had in her bag, she felt as if something transparent had pierced through the soft parts in the depths of her chest.

Her mind transported back to when she was seventeen.

*　　　*　　　*

After spending the night with Tamogami, accepting a business card with his contact information written on it, and parting at the station, Asuka had hurried back to Koumoto Books to look for *The Seagull*.

She had been curious to know what kind of girl Nina was and how Trigorin had destroyed her.

"You're like Nina in The Seagull.*"*

"So what will you do? I'll probably ruin you, you know."

She found *The Seagull* lined up on a shelf with Chekhov's other works, purchased it at the counter, and turned the pages with a pounding heart in the corner of a noisy fast-food restaurant.

The young and pure Nina, who dreams of being an actress, gets involved on a whim with Trigorin, a famous author, who considers their relationship nothing more than inspiration for a trifling short story.

Though Nina starts living with Trigorin in the city, love's hardships and jealousy wear her down, and she loses her confidence as an actress.

"I never knew what to do with my hands, I couldn't stand right, and voice control was beyond me. You can't possibly imagine what it's like to know you're awful on stage."

The person Nina is appealing to in that scene is not Trigorin, but a young man nicknamed Kostya, an old friend.

He is also an author and has always been in love with Nina, but Nina of course loves Trigorin.

Without so much as touching her cooling cup of coffee, seventeen-year-old Asuka read on breathlessly and swore she wouldn't turn out like the actress in *The Seagull*.

I'm not going to be tossed aside by Tamogami like Nina was. And I'm definitely going to succeed as an actress.

*   *   *

Thirty-six-year-old Asuka stretched out her hand toward the bookshelf, the memory of her painfully arrogant seventeen-year-old self gnawing at her breast.

She already knew all too well of the sadness and despair, hopes and prayers, and endless perseverance of the country-bred dreamer of a girl contained within that slim collection of plays.

When she pulled it off the shelf and held it in her hands, she noticed how incredibly smooth the cover was, how the pages weren't yellowed or warped at all. It was pretty, compared with the old copy of *The Seagull* that was in her bag. It was really pretty... Her throat quivered, her eyes blurred, and she nearly started crying.

Farther in, some housewives with children were gathered around a table, merrily writing on the display boards.

They looked about the same age as Asuka.

If I hadn't met Tamogami at that book signing at Koumoto Books—if I hadn't waited for him by the back door afterward, if I hadn't called out to stop him—I probably never would have gone to Tokyo, would I?

I would have graduated high school, stayed here and found a regular job, gotten married like everyone else, had a kid—I probably would have lived a happy life in a cozy little house, wouldn't I?

Had I never met him, I probably could have had that kind of happiness.

I would tell a funny story to my housewife friends and my family about how I wanted to be an actress long ago and be surprisingly content with that, wouldn't I?

All the mothers and children writing on their signs with multicolored markers and colored pencils looked so happy.

In this town, Asuka, who at thirty-six had still not achieved anything that could be called success as an actress nor even landed a steady job, Asuka, who was working in a hostess club, was a persona non grata.

This might be her hometown, but she couldn't step into that happy-looking circle.

She was sure that if any of her classmates from high school saw her now, they would ridicule her for being conceited enough to think she had been special. *You used to look down on us, but you're performing at underground theaters at age thirty-six—you can't exactly call yourself an actress, can you? And there's no way you're making a living that way, is there?*

Looking down at the glossy, brand-new copy of *The Seagull*, she felt as if she were about to burst from unhappiness and loneliness.

I want to go home.

This may be the place where I was born, but it's no longer the place I belong. I want to go back to Tokyo.

There, no one knew the seventeen-year-old me.

Why did I come here?
It's not like I can go back to being seventeen.

My Seagull *is all beat-up; it doesn't have any of this luster left; it's not beautiful anymore. The pages are creased and yellowed.*

Brand-new copy of *The Seagull* in hand, Asuka endured a stinging pain in her chest and stared at the ground.

"Asuka…?"

The voice of someone she had wanted to see so badly she could hardly stand it—but at the same time couldn't help but fear seeing—called out to her.

Her heart pounded loudly, and her whole body wound itself up tight.

When she looked up stiffly, she saw Tamogami standing there, wearing a trench coat over his suit, holding a designer business bag in one hand.

He had a bewildered expression on his face.

"I never expected to run into you… What are you up to these days?"

Asuka blinked away her tears and put on a smile just as if she were standing onstage.

"It's been a while, Tamogami. I had a feeling I would see you here. I'm acting in various roles in a small theater."

Surely Tamogami realized she couldn't be living off just that. He frowned sadly.

Am I really worn-out enough to force him into making such an awful face?

But wow, he's really aged.

He used to be full of confidence, a dazzling star.

Now he looks kinda distressed and lonesome.

Ah, that's it—this is exactly how he used to look when he drank too much and got depressed… But he never used to show this dour face outside.

"We're giving another public performance next month. My part is the second lead; it's quite a good role. Come and see the play if you want. I also perform at a club in Tsukiji, so if you're interested, you can come see me there, too. I'll get you in cheap, the ex-boyfriend special."

Asuka smiled again, wanting to convey to him that her life now was fulfilling. She tried to speak cheerfully.

The more wounded he looked, the more impatient she became. She tried to smile even more.

His gaze dropped to her hand.

He noticed the title of the book she was holding, grimaced, then mumbled something in a quiet voice.

"…*The Seagull*, huh? I knew it. I was Trigorin, and I ruined you…"

Asuka tried to smile again—and she couldn't.

Not only his words, but also the miserable look in his eyes pierced her heart.

"I'm completely exhausted! I want to rest for a moment—just rest!"

"I am—a seagull. No, that's not right…"

"A man who happened by saw a gull and killed it in a fit of boredom…"

"It could be an idea for a short story. No, that's not right…"

"What did I mean to say?"

Scraps of Nina's lines from when she was worn-out, tired, and hopeless reverberated in Asuka's mind.

If I hadn't met Tamogami, if I hadn't tried to get close to him, if I hadn't boarded the train to Tokyo—I'm having those thoughts again—

For a moment, an image of herself living happily without having ever met Tamogami—finishing high school, getting married in this town, having a child—ran through her mind...

Happily? Really?

No, that's not right!

The inside of Asuka's head flared up with heat, and she shouted in her heart. A strong feeling of outrage instantly seized her.

Nina's words that she had read aloud to herself over and over again, and the emotions and determination contained within, whirled up inside her mind. She felt as if she could hear the fluttering of bird wings.

Suddenly, she looked up and stared at Tamogami straight on. Then she spoke in an unwavering, powerful voice.

"You're wrong. I'm not ruined. Even if I had never met you and stayed in this town and gotten a job and gotten married and had a kid like everyone else, I would have regretted it. I would have constantly lamented that I wasn't being true to myself, and that what I really wanted to do was go to Tokyo to become an actress, and that I could have done it if I had gone when I was young. I wouldn't have been happy at all."

Tamogami's eyes opened wide.

He stared at Asuka as if he were seeing her for the first time.

"Thanks to you, I was able to become an actress. I've learned that I have to carry my own burdens. The reason I still keep acting, even now, is because *I want to.* I could have pursued a different life, but this is the path I've chosen. And I will continue to follow it into the future."

Right.
That's right.
Becoming an actress, even if I'm not famous at all, even if I never make it onto the big stage—continuing to act is something I do for myself.
I could have chosen countless other ways to live, but I didn't, because I couldn't stand living any other way.

"You're so strong," Tamogami mumbled.

There was no pity for Asuka left in his eyes or voice, just sadness and respect.

She laughed.

This time, it wasn't to hide her unhappiness. This time, she laughed to show her pride in herself.

"That's right—I am Nina after all.

"Acting or writing, it's all the same. The most important part of our jobs isn't the fame or the glory I once dreamed of. It's actually the strength to endure. That's what I've come to understand and believe.

"One should know how to bear one's own cross and have faith—it's true. Since I believe this, I don't suffer so much. When I think of my calling, I do not fear the life it led me to."

Asuka had never felt so much like Nina before.

Ah, I see.
I see—you were right, Nina.
I understand now.
There is still plenty of hardship and sorrow ahead of me, times when my life will feel empty and sad.

But despite all that, I am an actress.

*   *   *

And no matter what kind of past I've gone through or what kind of future I'm headed for, in this moment, right now, I can smile with strength and cheer.

"Good-bye, Tamogami. If you're so inclined, come and see a performance. I mean it."

With the new copy of *The Seagull* in hand and the old copy in her bag, Asuka turned her back on him and headed toward the register with both books.

The young employee with the glasses looked at her as she held out the glossy, new *Seagull*, and he grinned for some reason.

It was as if he had overheard the exchange between her and Tamogami.

Of course, there was no way he had, but she felt as if his smile was intended for her, and it felt good.

After paying, she asked, "This book and the old book I brought with me are the same title. Do you think I could get you to take a picture of me with them?"

The boy's grin was wide as he answered cheerily, "Yes, of course!" He looked charmed by the request, and with an excited expression, he added, "Right now, they'd really like to give you a hand! That's what these books are saying!"

"Wow, that's quite a reaction!" Asuka smiled, too.

Kind of an overreaction, but I'm happy for it.

"All right, smile!"

Holding the new *Seagull* in her right hand and the old *Seagull* in her left, Asuka squared her shoulders and smiled proudly.

That's right—I'm the flying bird Asuka.

A white seagull and an actress.

I'm going to keep moving forward, shouldering my burdens.

The boy with the glasses did a good job of taking the photo, and Asuka and her two *Seagulls* all came out beautifully.

Past, future, and present me!

*   *   *

She wrote out those words on a display, then headed over to the table with everyone else's handwritten signs and left hers there alongside them.

Bright, warm, joyous, pure, gentle, refreshed—the colorful boards were like a field of flowers, each one bearing a different emotion. And then—

—as if somehow compelled to, she found Tamogami's sign.

The accompanying photograph showed only the cover of a book, but the message scrawled across the sign was written in Tamogami's hand and had his signature.

As she was reading Tamogami's message, all the cheerful warmth quickly drained from Asuka's body, and she was struck by a terrible chill.

What should I do?

Icy fingers crawled up her spine, and her throat tightened with anxiety and fear.

Surely I'm overthinking it. I talked to Tamogami just a minute ago—his face was gloomy, but he didn't seem that tormented.

But then he's never been one to show his real feelings, even when we were living together—

"Ma'am, is something the matter?"

She had probably gone very pale.

The employee with the glasses had approached her unnoticed and addressed her with concern in his voice.

Staring directly at her, his big black eyes filled with earnest concern. It seemed as if he wanted to help Asuka however he could.

Without thinking, Asuka blurted out the dark worry swirling around in her heart.

"Please...don't let Tamogami out of your sight. I think he—*I think he might have come here to kill himself.*"

It had occurred to her that Tamogami wasn't really Trigorin, but actually Kostya, who despaired of life and, in the end, chose death.

Side Story

Together Forever
with *Kaiketsu
Zorori and the
Mysterious Aliens!*

Wow, there are so many customers!

After he was done with classes for the day, Hirotaka had gone to visit Koumoto Books with his own special volume in hand. When he saw how animated the interior of the shop was, he was filled with excitement.

From old men with white hair to children holding their mothers' hands to students wearing middle school uniforms like he was, people of all ages were gathered in the store, taking commemorative photographs and making colorful signs introducing their favorite books.

The completed pop signs hung everywhere throughout the shop, and the whole place had a bustling, festival-like atmosphere.

I felt depressed when I learned that Koumoto Books was going away soon, and I still feel really sad about it, but…

The town's one and only bookstore was special to Hirotaka.

He had first visited at this exact time of year nearly a decade ago, pulled along by the hand of his father. It was right after the huge earthquake that had rocked all of Tohoku.

At that time, Hirotaka had been a six-year-old kindergartner.

He had been playing with wooden blocks with a friend when suddenly a vibration pulsed from below, and their blocks had collapsed and scattered everywhere. After that, the whole building had jolted violently back and forth.

Hirotaka and the other children had started crying as their teacher instructed them in an urgent voice to take shelter under the desks.

But their young teacher had also never experienced such an enormous tremor, and it had been clear she was also confused and frightened.

The shaking continued for a long time, and Hirotaka held his head and cried under the desk.

He could hear things falling, smashing, and breaking against the floor. The incessant din scared him so much it was unbearable.

Whenever he thought the shaking was over, it would come again and again, Hirotaka crying all the while.

When his mother came to pick him up, he clung to her, bawling, and asked—

"Mama, did the earth break? I'm scared, so scared!"

Though she was pale like the kindergarten teacher, his mother embraced him tightly, her arms trembling.

That day, there were no lights in their home, so they turned on flashlights to illuminate the dark rooms and spent the night nearly freezing in the cold.

Small aftershocks and more powerful tremors occurred intermittently until morning, and Hirotaka clung to his mother all night, wrapped up in a blanket.

Electricity was restored the following day, but then Hirotaka was hit with a new round of shock and fear at the images of dark tsunami waves, murky floodwaters, crumbling buildings, and mountains of rubble that played on the television screen.

He wondered if those dark waves would swallow up his hometown as well.

He worried about his own house collapsing and being crushed, along with his mother and father inside it.

Instead of the cartoons and superhero shows that Hirotaka usually enjoyed every week, the television played an endless loop of footage showing the waves swallowing up towns. Even when he tried to change the channel with the remote, no matter what numbers he pushed and pushed and pushed, they all showed crumbling houses, the groaning and rumbling earth, and pitch-black waves.

Hirotaka spent the whole time crying, with a seating cushion over his head.

Worried, his father decided to take him on an outing.

"Hiro, come with Papa to the bookstore. I heard Koumoto Books is open, so I want to go buy some fun stuff to read there."

It hadn't even been three full days since the earthquake.

The area where Hirotaka lived had sustained only minor damage, and the essential utilities had been reconnected, but the shelves in the supermarket and convenience stores were empty. Everyone wore anxious, gloomy expressions and talked about how it would be best to evacuate far away in case another earthquake occurred.

Many of those voices reached Hirotaka's ears even though he was wearing fluffy earmuffs, so he gripped his father's hand tightly and hung his head.

I wonder if another earthquake is coming.

I wonder if we'll fall down and be buried under the rubble and die.

And I wonder if the pitch-black tsunami will swallow us up.

It seemed as if the tremors would come for them no matter where they ran, and Hirotaka felt as though he were being tossed about on a small boat in the middle of a storm.

His father took him to a bookstore in a slim three-story building.

"Wow, it's really open!"

Even now, in his third year of middle school, Hirotaka remembered clearly how his father's voice had shaken with emotion beside him.

He also recalled how his father had squinted his eyes, moved to tears.

At the time, he was a child and didn't understand it, but now he could imagine just how difficult it must have been to open a bookstore for business just three days after an earthquake. Like his father, the owner's determination moved Hirotaka, and he couldn't help but feel grateful.

Koumoto Books really helped us out back then.

Still being pulled by the hand by his father, Hirotaka had entered the shop and had seen a huge crowd of customers.

To his surprise, everyone was happily picking out books.

The people walking around town had been wearing sullen faces, crying and looking anxious, but here everyone was smiling cheerfully!

"Welcome!"

A kind-looking clerk with glasses greeted them calmly. When their eyes met, he grinned at little Hirotaka.

The other customers came up one after another to talk to the bespectacled clerk.

"Thank you so much for opening up the shop, Emon. In times like these, I want to read a ton of books."

"The TV is showing nothing but earthquake news on every channel. It's making me depressed. I really appreciate that Koumoto Books is open."

"Show me some books that'll make me smile, Emon."

"Give me a really exciting mystery that'll help me pass the time!"

The man whom they were calling Emon handled all the customers' inquiries with his eyes narrowed in a smile behind his glasses.

Inside the shop, the books that the earthquake had damaged were all piled up on sale for cheap, and people were happily picking them up.

Hirotaka's father also asked Emon about choosing a book his son would enjoy.

"He gets frightened whenever we turn on the TV and sits there shaking the whole time with a cushion on his head, poor kid. When I heard Koumoto Books was open, I thought we'd come look for something."

Emon frowned sadly, and tears formed at the corners of his eyes, but he quickly smiled again.

"I'm sorry to hear that. Well, thank you for coming."

Then he quickly bent down at the knee and looked Hirotaka in the eye.

"Hi there, how old are you?"

He asked his age.
Hirotaka kept his grip on his father's hand as he nervously answered.

"I'm...six."

Emon frowned sorrowfully again before scrunching up his face into a smile, then looking at Hirotaka with kind and tender eyes.

"I see. In the older class at kindergarten, are you? You're the same age as my kid. In that case, I have a recommendation."

He then showed Hirotaka and his father to the children's reading corner on the second floor.
There were lots of children there, noisily bustling about as they read books.
There was even a friend who went to the same kindergarten as Hirotaka.

*   *   *

"Ah, Hiro's here!"

Book in hand, the other child sunnily approached him.

"This book is suuuper fun! The owner suggested it."

He held it out with both hands, turning the cover toward Hirotaka.

On the cover was a fox wearing a black cloth mask over his eyes and a black hat on his head, riding in a rocket. From overhead, some strange green creature was sticking its face into the frame.

It looks like a really fun book.

Hirotaka read the title out loud.

"Kaiketsu Zorori…and the Mysterious Aliens?"

Emon was grinning.

"That's right, you read that so well! Your friend showed you before I could, but this is the book I recommend. My son, who's the same age as you, is a big fan of this series. The fox on the cover is named Zorori, and he's an outlaw, but he's also a good guy, and whenever people are in trouble, he helps them. He's friends with the boar twins Ishishi and Noshishi, and he travels around searching for a beautiful bride. Look here, these boars are Ishishi and Noshishi."

Emon pointed out the two boars, which were drawn in a comical style at the bottom of the cover.

"It's a long-running series, and they've published lots of volumes. If you like it, you can enjoy it for a long time."

After he explained, he brought over a copy of the same book that Hirotaka's friend had been holding.

*   *   *

"Start with this one. It's the tenth volume in the series, but they're written so that you can understand no matter where you start reading, so it'll be fine."

"We match!"

His friend from kindergarten thumped his book and Hirotaka's book together. Hirotaka also grinned widely and exclaimed back:

"Yeah, we match!"

This was the first time Hirotaka's father had seen his son smile since the earthquake, and he looked relieved.

While his father went down to the first floor to look for a book of his own, Hirotaka sat on the mat in the children's reading corner with his copy of *Kaiketsu Zorori and the Mysterious Aliens* that his father had just bought for him to read with his friend.

When he opened the cover, there was a drawing of a maze filling the whole two-page spread, with Ishishi and Noshishi the boars at the entrance and Zorori the fox standing at the exit wearing an umbrella hat and a cloak. Zorori had one hand up and was speaking in a manga-style speech bubble. His lines had a different font than the rest of the book.

"Hey! Get over here quick! We're camping out here!"

"Once Ishishi and Noshishi get to Zorori, then our story begins."

Just looking at the page made Hirotaka excited.

When he turned to the next page, Zorori and the boars were on a pleasant journey.

All the kanji and katakana characters had their readings written out plainly, so even six-year-old Hirotaka was able to read easily.

Just like on that first page, the words Zorori and his friends spoke were sometimes in speech bubbles, mixed in with the regular prose text. It was super easy to read! And so fun!

Along their journey, Zorori and his party discover a "crop circle."

On the page was a mysterious design with one big circle enclosing four smaller circles, drawn in a sweet potato field.

"Eek! Noshishi, that's a crop circle—I'm sure of it!"

"A crop circle? What's that? Is it good to eat?"

"You two wouldn't know anything about it. All right, I'll explain it to you!"

On the next page, there was an easily understandable layout with a detailed explanation of the phenomenon, along with the headline "What Are Crop Circles?" Hirotaka read through that, too, his heart pumping with excitement.

When Noshishi and Ishishi try to pull up potatoes from the field, a UFO appears, and Noshishi gets sucked up into the spaceship, still clinging to a long, skinny sweet potato. Illustrated across another two-page spread that read from top to bottom, Zorori assembles a rocket in a flash and blasts off into space to save Noshishi.

When Zorori and Ishishi arrive at the star where the green aliens live, they have to take many strange intelligence tests to save Earth from the aliens, along with solving some puzzles. They have to contend with alien creatures, and they fall in love at first sight with an alien princess.

The story sped right along.

This is fun, so much fun!

While immersed in the pages, Hirotaka completely forgot about how frightened he had been of the earthquake.

There was a somewhat large tremor as he was reading, and his father anxiously went up to the second floor to check on him, but Hirotaka hadn't noticed the shaking and was still reading *Mysterious Aliens*.

Because the owner, Emon, recommended this book to me back then, I read Mysterious Aliens *every day and didn't have a spare second to be afraid. It's a fun and exciting read.*

After reading over and over and over the first book my dad bought for me, I went with my mom to buy a different volume of Zorori. Emon remembered me and asked how I liked the book.

"Was it interesting?"

"Suuuuuuper interesting!"

Hirotaka answered with bright red cheeks, and in response, Emon smiled kindly, his eyes narrowing behind his glasses.

"In that case, how about this one next? Zorori makes ramen in it."

He recommended a book titled *Kaiketsu Zorori, It's Hot! A Ramen Showdown*, which had Zorori drawn on the cover eating a delicious-looking bowl of ramen.

The illustration was amusing, and the ramen looked so tasty that Hirotaka's mouth began to water. His appetite, which had been absent since the earthquake, immediately returned.

"Mama, I want to eat ramen!"

Before he had even finished reading the book to the end, he was pestering his mother.

In this way, once he had savored each volume to his heart's content, Hirotaka would ask to go back to Koumoto Books, where he would get Emon to pick out the next book in the Zorori series for him to read. The bookshelf in his room at home held every volume in the whole lineup before he knew it.

Even nine years after that, the Zorori series was still ongoing. Whenever a new book came out, Hirotaka enjoyed visiting Koumoto Books and chatting with Emon.

Once, when Hirotaka had entered middle school and had visited the shop wearing his new school uniform, Emon had smiled, almost overcome with emotion.

"Ah, that's right... Little Hirotaka is already a middle school student..."

His eyes were deeply kind as always as he gazed at him—and Hirotaka, who knew about Emon's circumstances, found it just a little painful.

As far as Hirotaka was concerned, he owed a debt of gratitude to Emon.

If Emon hadn't opened up his shop three days after the earthquake, and if his father hadn't taken Hirotaka with him to Koumoto Books—he might still be living in fear of earthquakes to this day.

Once he had read the whole Zorori series, he had a realization.

Emon had been very careful to avoid recommending any books that depicted buildings collapsing or flooding. He had chosen books he knew wouldn't frighten Hirotaka.

Now Hirotaka was able to separate such depictions from his earthquake experience and enjoy those other volumes, but at the time, he would definitely have been too frightened to keep reading.

Empathizing closely with the feelings of the reader and selecting just the right book—not only was Emon truly great at running his bookstore, but he was also an extremely sensitive and kind individual.

Not to mention a strong person.

He'd said he had opened his shop so quickly after the earthquake because he'd known that, in times of crisis, there would be many people who would need books for comfort and support.

He truly believed books had that power. In that moment, there was something he could do as a bookseller for the sake of those people. And he had followed through on that.

Hirotaka had been surprised to learn much later that Emon's wife and son had died in the earthquake.

The child Emon had said was the same age as Hirotaka was a long-awaited son. They had been blessed with the boy after his sickly wife had all but given up on having children, and Emon cherished and treasured him.

"He looked just like Emon and was the cutest little thing. He always said that, when he grew up, he was going to run the bookstore just like his papa!"

The regular who'd told Hirotaka about it had been tearing up as she spoke.

The day of the earthquake, Emon's son had gone to spend time at his wife's family home near the seashore, and there the waves had swallowed up his child along with his wife and her family.

That was the reason why Emon had looked so terribly sad when he'd heard Hirotaka's age. As he spoke to Hirotaka, he had been imagining his dead son.

After losing his wife and child in one fell swoop, he'd immediately opened up the shop and had smiled with such a serene expression on his face.

How was he able to do that?

What could he have been thinking when he'd just been left alone in the world?

When he was in the shop, Emon always smiled as he gave advice to his customers and spent the day pleasantly conversing about books. He never let it show that something so tragic had happened to him.

How truly kind and resilient he was.

I never thought he'd leave us so soon.

And so suddenly.

And I couldn't have ever imagined that Koumoto Books would close down.

The townspeople had been wondering if there might be someone who could purchase the bookstore and become the new owner, and a few residents had even been making inquiries, but the circumstances were apparently more complicated than that.

If Koumoto Books closed, the bookstores would disappear from the town.

It was a sad thought, but Hirotaka was a middle school student and couldn't do anything about it.

Besides, something felt wrong about the store continuing on without Emon.

As far as I'm concerned, Koumoto Books was Emon.

If Emon is gone, then Koumoto Books is also finished.
Surely that's only right.

"Hiro, you're so heartless! How can you accept this so easily? I just can't stand the thought that the shop is closing!

When Hirotaka had declined to sign his friend's petition to keep Koumoto Books open, his friend had gotten mad, and they had argued about it.

"It's not that simple! It was upsetting for me to hear that it's disappearing, too. But to me, a Koumoto Books without Emon is not Koumoto Books at all."

"So you're saying you're fine with it closing?!"

"I never said it was fine. Just, I think keeping it open would be wrong."

"I don't get you at all. You jerk."

His friend didn't talk to him for three days.
You're the jerk, Souta. I'm super torn up that Koumoto Books is closing, too, you know.
Today Hirotaka had come alone, to say his good-byes to Emon.
Just as it had been after the earthquake, the inside of the shop was lively, and lots of customers were happily picking out books.
There were old men, housewives, young women, students, and young children.
Everyone was smiling.
Emon sold books with a smile to make everyone happy, even when he himself was sad and suffering.

So I'm going to smile, too, and say farewell to Emon and Koumoto Books.
I'm sure that's what he would have wanted.

"Welcome!"

A clerk wearing big glasses who looked about high school age shouted a cheerful greeting.

Hirotaka had never seen him before, but the clerk's eyes were twinkling, and his expression was friendly and bright.

"We're holding our store's grand closing sale at the moment. Did you happen to bring with you a book that is connected to memories of this shop?"

"Yes! I brought a book that Emon chose for me—one that I loved most of all!"

Hirotaka also answered energetically.

When he pulled *Kaiketsu Zorori and the Mysterious Aliens* out of his bag and held it up high, the clerk with the glasses narrowed his eyes softly like Emon used to do and looked over the cover slowly and deliberately.

It was almost as if he was greeting the book.

He looked at it with kind eyes, full of affection and respect.

His mouth slowly broke into a smile.

And he mumbled in satisfaction.

"Ah…how wonderful. Your book seems very happy."

The other clerk working next to him shot him a sidelong scowl, but he just smiled.

Hirotaka also didn't understand what he meant and was stunned for a moment, but he was happy to have someone who resembled Emon tell him that. He felt a little embarrassed.

"Thank you very much. Um, could I get you to take my photo as well? I want to get a picture and write a display!"

"Sure! All right then, stand over here with your friend."

"Huh?"

When Hirotaka turned around to follow the gaze of the bespectacled clerk, he saw another boy wearing the same middle school uniform as him, standing there awkwardly.

He was holding *Kaiketsu Zorori, It's Hot! A Ramen Showdown* in front of his chest.

My friend Souta!

It was the boy whose petition to keep Koumoto Books open Hirotaka had declined to sign, the one with whom he had been quarreling—

Why is he here?

When I tried to invite him to come, he refused.

He's also got a book from the same series.

Hey, you, your face is red—well, mine probably is, too. I'm burning up.

Both boys were fidgeting, each trying to guess how the other would react. The clerk with the glasses spoke up in a clear, cheerful voice.

"I'm sure both of you must have some really wonderful memories of Koumoto Books! You both feel the same way about this place, and your books are saying together, 'Hurry and make up!' Besides, that's what Emon would want, right?"

It's not like our books are actually talking!

But since the clerk had brought up the owner's name, Hirotaka and Souta couldn't very well continue their argument here.

After they each checked the other's expression again, Hirotaka readied himself for whatever might happen and walked over to Souta.

Souta opened his eyes wide as Hirotaka thumped his book into the Zorori volume he was holding and smiled slightly. Then, just like back when the two of them excitedly read *Mysterious Aliens* while sitting on the mat in the children's corner of Koumoto Books after the earthquake, Hirotaka said:

"…We match, huh?"

Souta stuck his lip out a little as he answered bluntly:

"Yeah, we match."

The boys bumped their books together as they had nine years earlier.

Maybe back then, Hirotaka's and Souta's books shouted something like:

"That hurts!"

And complained about the rough treatment.

Book
3

The
Sins of
The
Scarlet
Letter

"—Didn't he… Didn't Emon Koumoto die because of me?"

Tamogami hung his head, face warped with anguish and at his wit's end. He sounded extremely distressed.

"Just let me die, please. I can't take it anymore."

Kouichi Tamogami first met Emon when the latter had just become the third owner of Koumoto Books. Kanesada, the second owner, had died of a sudden illness. That was before Tamogami had debuted as an author. Back then, he was working at city hall, in an intolerably irritating job where he had to listen carefully to every little trivial matter (or so they seemed to him) that the residents brought before him.

He had always gotten good grades, and in middle and high school, he had never fallen below fifth place in the class rankings posted in the hallways. Despite his grades, his economic situation meant that his only option for continuing his education was commuting to the local community college while living at home with his parents. He was quite dissatisfied with this arrangement.

I really should have gone to one of the top universities in Tokyo, gotten hired by some distinguished corporation, and landed some glamorous international job, and yet…

What am I doing in this tiny town hall, listening to the ramblings of the elderly, bobbing my head like some peon?

He would vent this frustration through his writing. In those days, he spent all his time writing novels to submit to contests.

I'll get prize money if I win.

Then I'll go to Tokyo.

If my book sells, I'll be rich and famous. Then I'll be able to gloat over all those losers who went to good schools in Tokyo despite being dumber than me.

While he was working in town hall, he wrote his manuscripts using a special fountain pen meant for just that task at a pace of one book every four months. However, they never took higher than third place in any competition.

What can I do to improve?

If I've got the skills to make it to third place, the rest is just luck.

So how can I nudge my luck in the right direction?

Tamogami would get stressed out whenever the results of a "new writer" award were announced.

One time, on the eve of an announcement, he found himself striking up a conversation with the shopkeeper at Koumoto Books, where he often had books on layaway.

The shopkeeper with the glasses and the kind face was one year younger than him and had a gentle personality.

He understood how to talk to people without making them uncomfortable and was very supportive of Tamogami, who always felt better after chatting with the younger man.

That was Emon, who had lost his mother early in life and had spent his time reading books in the shop for as long as he could remember. He had a deep enough knowledge of every genre to astonish even Tamogami, who normally took great pride in being well-read.

And yet, Emon never used this unstudied, superior knowledge as a tool to make others look foolish or to make himself look better. He was always modest and relaxed when he spoke.

In those days, when the internet was not as developed as it is now, having someone in this small Tohoku town with whom he could have a meaningful discussion was precious to Tamogami.

He visited Koumoto Books even on days when he had no plans to purchase anything, just so that he could enjoy talking about literature and creative writing with Emon.

There was an office in the back, past the children's reading corner on the second floor, and the two of them often conversed through the night there. Sometimes Emon's wife, Yaeko, would peek her head in and bring them something to eat.

"It's a relief you're caught up discussing literature with Tamogami rather than drinking yourself unconscious in a pub somewhere. But everything's best in moderation, you know."

There was a bookshelf lined with many different volumes in the small, concrete room. All of them were Emon's private property. He said they were his favorites. Besides those, the blue trunk alongside the wall was where he stored books that were damaged or old but were still important enough that he wanted to keep them.

Above the trunk hung a peculiar painting. It depicted a blue ocean and a gray sandy beach littered with the bones of some huge bird. The bones were a bright, almost sublime white, and they stood out against the sea and sand.

The image was stark and desolate, but it nevertheless captivated everyone who looked at it.

"My father painted that."

Kanesada, the second-generation owner, was a true Renaissance man, friendly and handsome and popular—apparently, he would have actually preferred to have been an actor or a painter rather a bookseller.

"That's why I took over for him so early. I always wanted to see my dad get to do what he loved in life. I would run the store so he could become a painter. When I was a kid, I pinkie promised that if we did that, he could sell collections of his paintings in the shop…"

*   *   *

Emon smiled softly, his voice somewhat bittersweet because Kanesada had met his end before he could fulfill his promise.

A chill shot down Tamogami's spine when he heard that the title of the painting was *Extinction*.

I guess Emon's father died with regrets, never becoming the man he wanted to be?

He imagined himself facing the same fate and suddenly found it difficult to breathe.

Tamogami had been keeping his manuscripts a secret. Emon was the one and only person in whom he had confided the ambitions roiling in his heart. In response, Emon had smiled gently and given Tamogami a gratifying answer.

"Your novels are clever and very interesting, Kouichi, so I'm sure you'll win someday. When you do, please hold a book signing here at Koumoto Books."

Tamogami boasted to his friend.

"Sure, I will. I'll make the line wrap around the block."

Emon narrowed his eyes in a smile, as if he couldn't wait for that day to come.

"I'm looking forward to it."

But even after that, Tamogami's novels still couldn't seem to do better than third place. His days of frustration continued.

It was especially irritating whenever the winner was younger than him. His eyes would be nearly burning as he glared at the pen name of the winner published in the magazine. His throat would dry out, and his hands would shake.

Why not me? Why is it this guy?! He's three years younger than me! That's bullshit!

He couldn't help but curse everything.

I'd rather go extinct than live in a world where I can never win.

Staring intensely at the painting titled *Extinction* and imagining a world in which all living things had died out and turned into piles of bones only intensified his anger.

Even at times like that, Emon would look at Tamogami with clear eyes and carefully encourage him, selecting words that wouldn't damage his pride.

"Kouichi, you've got plenty of talent to make a strong debut, so I think all that's left is to choose a good subject. Maybe the themes in the works you've submitted so far were a little too complicated."

Emon's words calmed Tamogami's heart, as if he were listening to the peaceful murmurings of a river.

But later, when he was alone in his room at home facing his pad of paper, all the frustration and impatience and jealousy welled up again. He tore up the sheets of his unfinished draft, balled up the paper, and threw it violently to the floor.

You say my themes are too esoteric, so tell me what I should write instead!

One day, he told Emon he no longer knew what to write about.

"How about some tea?"

Emon invited Tamogami to his office on the second floor where they always talked after the store was closed. But that day, they convened during business hours. Tamogami must have looked as if he was at the end of his rope if the bookseller was inviting him up so much earlier in the day.

Emon was great at making tea.

When Tamogami took a sip of the slightly sweet Chinese blend that Emon had slowly poured from a small teapot into the prewarmed teacup, his dry throat was moistened, and his stomach gradually warmed up.

*   *   *

"Relax in here; read a book."

Emon said that and left.

After he was gone, Tamogami pondered what topics would appeal to the masses as he gazed vacantly at the shelf full of assorted books.

Then, on the edge of the shelf, he spotted a handmade pamphlet.

The slim volume was sandwiched between two sheets of cardboard, with holes punched through and bound together with string—it looked just like something a child would make during an arts and crafts class.

When he pulled it off the shelf, he saw there was a title written on the front cover in light-blue crayon.

The Last Bookstore.

Something about it captured his interest, and he opened the cover.

Inside was a picture of a building that looked like a bookstore, drawn in crayon.

"There was only one bookstore in the town.

"Once there had been three, but one by one, they closed, until finally the last one was all alone."

The childish writing explained that the owner of the bookstore was very old, and one day when he was behind the counter, sitting in a chair, he passed away in his sleep. The old man had no family, so it was decided that the bookstore would close.

"On the day of the funeral, the people of the town gathered at the bookstore.

"Everyone brought a book that held special memories for them.

* * *

"And they told one another about their favorites.

"Each person made a sign about their title.

"The signs were many colors—pink, red, blue, yellow, purple—and all together, they looked like a field of flowers."

Before Tamogami knew it, he was utterly fixated, almost forgetting to breathe.

The writing and illustrations were crude, like a child's.
But this—
His heart was pounding hard.
His chest was painfully hot.
Yes, this is it—

◇   ◇   ◇

"Tamogami is a Kostya pretending to be a Trigorin! He's going to try to kill himself!"
A woman clutching to her chest two copies of *The Seagull*—one old and worn and the other brand-new—was insisting upon this with a desperate expression.
Stunned, Minami begged to know what the woman was talking about so abruptly.
Trigorin and Kostya are both characters in *The Seagull*. The heroine Nina is in love with Trigorin, a writer and a much older man of about her father's age who comes to visit from the capital. Ultimately, Trigorin leaves Nina behind.
Kostya is the pet name for a man named Konstantin Treplev, a youth about Nina's age. He and Nina used to be in love before her affections shifted to Trigorin.
Though Kostya becomes a writer, too, he despairs of the profession and

feels hopeless about himself. Unable to see a way forward, he commits suicide after reuniting with Nina.

Koumoto Books was right in the middle of its grand closing sale, which
meant that lots of customers had come to visit the shop, and Minami and
the other staff were incredibly busy.

Despite all that, the boy with glasses, the temporary part-timer who had
barged in without an invitation, had willfully left his post and wandered off
somewhere. *He's probably planning to give some nonsensical excuse again, like*
The books were calling to me *or whatever.* A sour look painted on her face,
Minami went searching for him and found him deep in a serious-looking
discussion with a beautiful and neatly appointed woman in the literature
section on the first floor.

The woman seemed to be in her late twenties. Her attire was plain, but
her makeup and nails were flashy and eye-catching.

"—Ah, Ms. Tsuburaya, we've got trouble!"

His eyes were round with panic. According to both the uninvited
employee Enoki and the beautiful lady holding two copies of *The Seagull*,
the author Kouichi Tamogami was going to commit suicide, so they wanted
to keep an eye on him.

Tamogami was a novelist who grew up in the area and was a friend of the
store's late owner. Long ago, he had also held a book signing at Koumoto
Books. Minami had used the store computer to send an e-mail notice of
the owner's passing to the address for a Mr. Tamogami. She had ended the
message by asking him to come to the store's grand closing sale if he was
able.

But at that point, he had been declining requests relating to his hometown for many years and hadn't even returned for the reconstruction of the
area after the earthquake, so Minami hadn't expected anything.

She'd also heard from the old part-timer who had quit the previous
year that Tamogami had turned down invitations from Emon as well.
The owner would get depressed over it and complain that Tamogami was
heartless...

And yet, about an hour earlier, a handsome middle-aged man wearing a trench coat and carrying a designer business bag had entered the shop, presented a business card at the register, and introduced himself.

"I once had the privilege of holding a book signing here. I received your kind e-mail. Please accept my condolences for your loss."

Even without looking at the card, Minami knew this was the author Kouichi Tamogami. There was a photo hanging up from when he held his signing in the shop.

The photo was nearly twenty years old and Tamogami had aged since then, but even now, his handsome build hadn't changed that much.

It's really him!

There was no one in this town who wouldn't recognize him, and the fact that the bestselling author was in their shop had all the other employees excited.

Minami showed him through to the office and left the room to go prepare tea. When she came back with a cup of tea on a tray, the business bag with the brand logo on it was sitting on the side table, and he was still standing, staring at the painting on the wall.

A blue ocean, gray sand, huge bird bones—it was the picture Kanesada, the store's second owner, had painted and titled *Extinction*.

Tamogami was frowning, looking very sad and tormented, and Minami hesitated to say anything.

As she stood there, Tamogami noticed her instead, and his mouth curved awkwardly, as if he was trying to smile and failing. He mumbled—

"So this painting is still here, huh?"

"Yes. It's a memento of the owner's father."

"That's right. Kanesada painted it before he died."

Once Tamogami had finished his tea, he stood up from the sofa and picked up his bag, not seeming to want to stay too long.

*   *   *

"It's been a long time since I was here, so I'd like to take a good, long look around and think fondly of the departed."

That's what he'd said. And he'd added that she needn't fuss over him any further.

He had seemed as if he didn't want any to-do over the fact that someone famous had shown up, so Minami reassured him.

"I understand. If you need anything, please let me know."

She saw Tamogami off outside the office.

Then she returned to the first floor and cautioned the other part-timers not to pester him for signatures or anything. But Musubu, the person she was most concerned about, hadn't been around at the time, so she had told herself she would have to give him a warning later.

But what he was saying when she found him talking to the beautiful lady, away from his post, was unthinkable—that Tamogami had come to the shop to commit suicide.

The attractive woman, who had a very cosmopolitan air about her, said she and Tamogami used to live together.

That might have been true, but Minami was skeptical. Maybe she was a passionate fan of his, or possibly even a stalker. She thought Musubu was out of his mind for believing something so dubious.

Well, he has said from the beginning that he can hear the words of books, and he did introduce me to a slim book with a blue cover and told me it was his "girlfriend." He's been awfully, undeniably strange *this whole time, but...*

In short, Minami concluded she did not have the time to listen seriously to the silly talk of this suspicious customer and strange employee when things were so busy. But—

"What Asuka is saying is true. The books in this area are also making a commotion. They say Mr. Tamogami was acting strangely, like he might be in danger or something."

More weirdness from Musubu.

Of course, she couldn't hear any such commotion in the least.

But the big eyes staring at her from behind his glasses were the very definition of earnest—

Besides that, when she thought back on the things she'd witnessed over these past few days since Musubu had come to Koumoto Books— she couldn't deny she had thought several times that maybe he *could* hear something after all...

Asuka Kanno, the woman standing next to Musubu wearing a strained expression and who was Tamogami's supposed former live-in partner, chimed in.

"Look at this."

She thrust a paper sign toward Minami.

It had Tamogami's signature on it and a photo of the man holding a book.

"The Scarlet Letter"...?

It was a work of American literature about an incident of adultery that takes place in Puritan society in seventeenth-century Boston.

This is what he picked?

She recalled their exchange in the office.

"We borrowed the idea of having customers write pop signs at our closing sale from A Funeral for Kanoyama Books. *Please write one of your own if you'd like, Mr. Tamogami. Of course, a sign about your own novel would be very warmly received. I know that the owner also loved your book. He always said that* A Funeral for Kanoyama Books *was special."*

For just a moment, Tamogami's eyes went dark again. Then he smiled.

"I see... Well, I wonder what I should write."

Minami had been certain he had written his display about his signature work, *A Funeral for Kanoyama Books*.

But The Scarlet Letter?

If I remember correctly, it's about a woman who conceives and bears a child after an illicit affair while her husband is missing. She's put in the stocks and has a large, red letter A sewn to her clothing, marking her as an "adulteress," and has to live with the judgment of her community... Despite all that, the woman absolutely refuses to name her partner in the affair.

On the other hand, the child's father, a minister named Dimmesdale, weakens day by day from guilt, until finally he confesses his crime on the same stocks where they made the woman stand and dies on the spot.

Why did Tamogami choose that book, of all things?

The hasty handwriting on his display read:

Dimmesdale died because he couldn't bear the pressure of the crime he'd kept secret for so long. The guilt killed him, but it saved him at the same time.

Even Minami felt a little jolt race up her spine.

"Death saved him."

The other customers wrote about either their favorite part of the book they brought or a section that influenced their life, or they included some reminiscence about Koumoto Books. Almost all the content on the signs is positive, but this...

Still holding the display out toward Minami with an intense look in her eye, Asuka spoke in a frantic voice.

"Tamogami felt very guilty about something to do with Emon. I don't know why exactly, but when we were living together, whenever there was some communication from Emon, he always looked very upset. And I also heard him address Emon in his sleep. He would say things like 'Please forgive me... Please help me...' When he was sleep-talking, Tamogami would get drenched in sweat, and his face would twist up; he would choke himself with his own hands and groan. I would shake him awake desperately, afraid that he was going to actually stop breathing. No matter how I asked, he never talked to me about what had happened between him and Emon.

But for nearly twenty years—maybe even longer—Tamogami has wanted to die."

Asuka's words, like surging waves, frightened Minami. She could feel her pulse quicken.

Mr. Tamogami wanted to die?

He felt guilty toward the boss?

Tried to choke himself with his own hands?

The lines scribbled on the pop sign did indeed have an ominous air to them. They kept flashing through her mind.

The guilt killed him, but it saved him at the same time.

Death saved him.

"Tamogami—he wanted to be saved! Then Emon passed away, and the only person he could ask for forgiveness was gone. Because of that, he fixated on the thought that he had no way out but to die as well, and he probably chose Koumoto Books as the place to do it!"

Asuka's words struck Minami's ears and sent her head spinning.

There's no way! Asuka's worrying too much.

But it's true that until today, Mr. Tamogami had never once visited Koumoto Books after his book signing and that he and the boss were estranged—

When Minami had once proposed getting Mr. Tamogami to hold another book signing, Emon had looked a little sad as he replied.

"Kouichi is a busy man. I wonder if he would."

There had been something dark in his eyes.

Minami had wondered if something had happened between them.

"Mr. Tamogami is a Tokyo person now, so he wants to cut ties with the people from his hometown. He was such good friends with Emon; it's a real shame.

The only time he's called was to give his condolences when Emon lost his wife and child."

An elderly part-timer had complained to Minami about how utterly heartless the author had been. After that, she'd avoided the topic of Kouichi Tamogami in the store.

As she recalled those things now, Minami found it hard to breathe.

"...I don't know whether he's trying to kill himself, but let's find him and hear what he has to say for the time being. Is that all right?"

Minami asked this in a steady voice, and Asuka nodded.

"Yes, thank you. I'll help look for him, too."

"All right, we'd better hurry. I have a feeling this is a very dangerous situation, based on what the books have to say."

Asuka paled at Musubu's words, and Minami glared at him.

"Enoki, that's uncalled for. Also, if you find Mr. Tamogami, don't blurt out *Did you come here to kill yourself?* or something stupid like that. Tell him *We'd like to speak with you* and show him into the office."

"Okay, roger!" he answered and instantly took off running.

"Hey—don't run!"

By the time she shouted after him, his small back and gently bouncing black hair were already quite far away.

Good grief!

Scowl on her face, Minami also set out to search for Tamogami.

It looked as if Musubu had run up to the second floor, so Minami entrusted the third floor to Asuka and looked around the first floor herself.

She asked the other part-timers if any of them had seen Tamogami, but she only got information she already knew.

"I saw him writing on a display sign earlier. Hawthorne's *The Scarlet Letter* is a pretty grim choice, don't you think?"

"I noticed him talking with a beautiful female customer. The woman seemed to be crying a little bit. It sure looked like a lovers' quarrel. Maybe they were old sweethearts reunited or something. Just what you would expect from a handsome bestselling author, huh?"

Minami made a circuit around the sales floor and concluded that he probably wasn't on the first floor… Then, just as she was thinking that, her cell phone started vibrating in her pocket.

It was a call from Musubu.

"Ms. Tsuburaya, I found Mr. Tamogami. He's in the second-floor toilets. Please come quickly!"

His voice was panicked, and he was speaking faster than usual. Minami broke into an anxious run, taking the stairs to the second floor two at a time and heading for the bathrooms.

They were located beside the office and split off into men's and women's rooms on the inside.

A triangular CLEANING IN PROGRESS sign stood at the entrance.

Musubu must have put this here.

The door with the men's symbol on it was propped open, and Minami was startled to find a person slumped over the toilet. Red blood was trickling from his wrists, forming a pool of crimson on the floor.

It was Tamogami!

Someone was crouched over him, but it wasn't Musubu. For some reason, the veterinarian Michijirou was there, holding Tamogami's other hand and checking his pulse.

Then Musubu came bursting in, carrying a first aid kit.

"Mr. Michijirou, please help!"

He opened the kit and handed it to him.

"You asked for a doctor, but I'm a vet, you know…"

He grumbled as he tended to Tamogami. Minami squeezed her own left wrist, which had begun throbbing with pain, with her right hand—and trembled as she watched.

Though the blood loss was considerable, the wound was shallow, so it turned out that Tamogami's life was not seriously at risk.

He'd probably lost consciousness due to lack of sleep and fatigue, Michijirou told them once he had finished his emergency measures.

*   *   *

"I went to use the bathroom, but there was someone in there before me, so I waited outside. I was just thinking that he was taking a long time, when Enoki here came running up all red in the face and started busting open the lock with a crowbar. My, was I surprised!"

Musubu smiled and said what he had been saying all along.

"The books told me. I'm glad I got here in time."

Musubu and Michijirou, along with Asuka, whom Musubu had called down to help, carried Tamogami from the bathroom into the adjacent office and laid him down on the sofa.

Minami just stood there trembling. There wasn't anything she could do.

Most people who knew her thought of her as a stable, grounded sort of person, and that was how she saw herself as well. Yet her own left wrist had started pulsing with stabbing pain the instant she saw the blood streaming from Tamogami's limp wrist, and she hadn't been able to stop herself from shivering and shaking.

Pathetic.

But she was still shuddering, remembering the scene.

When she thought about what would have happened if Tamogami died, she was helpless to prevent the trembling from creeping in.

"Ms. Tsuburaya, I'll lock up the shop, so please go home and get some rest. After all, tomorrow will be another busy day. We'll be in trouble if we lose our leader," Musubu suggested, apparently out of concern for Minami.

Then, as if the "girlfriend" in his pocket had said something to him, he made an excuse: "No, it's not cheating! I'm just worried about a coworker, that's all."

"...I'm fine. The store manager can't possibly go home after something like this has happened."

There were four people in the office at the moment: Minami, Musubu, Asuka, and Tamogami.

The store was getting ready to close for the night, and the shutters had been pulled down. All the other part-timers had gone home. Minami hadn't told any of them about Tamogami.

She had said she was staying out of a sense of responsibility as their leader and for her own pride. But she also really wanted to know what had transpired between Tamogami and Emon.

What has been tormenting Tamogami so?

And for that matter, what happened twenty years ago?

Tamogami wrote that "the guilt killed him."

Just what kind of crime did this guy commit against the boss?

Still unconsciously gripping her aching left wrist with her right hand while listening to the clock on the wall tick away the minutes, Minami thought back to when she had been an easily frightened coward.

She had been afraid, so afraid, of everything around her—she had been terrified of nightfall. She was thin, skin and bones really, and her face was covered in acne. She couldn't look people in the eye and always hung her head—that was the Minami for whom Emon had poured the sweet roasted green tea, here in this place.

Just like now, back then the painting of the discarded bird bones by the seashore hung on the wall, with the blue storage box below. On the shelf were miscellaneous books of all sizes and genres.

Classics, contemporary literature, mysteries, poetry anthologies, art books, books about mountaineering and fishing, soccer, law, politics, cookbooks…

All of them belonged to the owner.

But Emon, who had stood in front of the shelf with his eyes narrowed in a gentle smile, was no more.

Minami would never again see the man who had helped her that day, could no longer hear his voice or ask him to pour her sweet tea again.

He's gone.

The air that filled the small gray room felt different than it had back then. It was heavy and sad, and it smelled like death.

How can I get this shaking to stop?

I wonder if we can clear out the anxiety and dreariness hanging over this room.

Even the memory of Emon's face smiling at her from across a steaming cup of tea seemed to grow steadily more sorrowful and lonesome. He had never said anything about being lonely or having a hard time.

Minami realized she had never known how he was truly feeling.

I knew—nothing.

"…Enoki, you can hear the voices of books, right? In that case, tell me something. How did the boss spend his time in this room when he was alone? He was all by himself for quite a while after losing his wife and child. Wasn't he lonely?"

She had been adamant this whole time that there was no way Musubu could speak with books. Minami also envied the boy, to whom Emon had entrusted the store's inventory.

Geez, the stress must be getting to me…

There were too many things happening at once, and her mental processing power wasn't able to keep up. She didn't know what she should do.

That's why she asked Musubu this very silly question.

"…I think he was lonely," he answered in a kind voice. "Both of his parents passed away when he was young, and then he suddenly lost his wife and child at once in a natural disaster, so there's no way he wasn't lonely. But he wasn't alone. He had lots of books and all the part-time workers and the customers who came to see him… When taken as a whole, everything that made up Koumoto Books was Emon's family—I'm sure of it."

Baby-faced Musubu was younger than Minami, and his figure hadn't filled out yet—he was still in high school. So why was he able to speak in this gentle voice that seemed to speak straight to her heart?

She felt on the verge of tears just listening to him…

But it would be embarrassing if she cried now, so she resisted with all her might.

Asuka, who was attending to Tamogami next to the sofa, also looked as if she was tearing up a little as he spoke.

Then she muttered, "Ah!"

Tamogami had opened his eyes.

Minami and Musubu turned toward the sofa eagerly.

He cracked open his eyes slightly, staring vacantly for a moment at Asuka peering down at him.

But eventually, he winced, mumbling hopelessly, "...So I couldn't even manage to die, huh? Even though Emon...he died because of me..."

Minami was taken aback.

Asuka pressed him for more.

"What do you mean, Emon died because of you?"

"Because I...committed a crime... I succumbed to temptation... I never thought I would suffer so much for it..."

He kept on grumbling bitterly without getting to the point at all.

Even this late in the game, he seemed hesitant to make his crime public. But then—

"Mr. Tamogami, you wrote that Reverend Dimmesdale in *The Scarlet Letter* died because he couldn't stand the stress of keeping his crime a secret, right? The guilt killed him, and it saved him at the same time, you said. That may have been true. But your salvation is not in death. Yours lies in confessing that which you feel is a crime."

Tamogami turned to look at Musubu, and his eyes went wide.

"...Emon?"

His lips moved slightly as he mumbled his old friend's name, looking as if he had seen a ghost.

It must have been because of the glasses. When he looked at Musubu, Tamogami must have seen his deceased friend. He sat up and strained his eyes.

But soon an expression rose on his face that was a mixture of disappointment and self-deprecation.

"Ah, that's right... Emon is dead..."

Covering his face with one hand, he shook his head back and forth.

Still, Musubu appealed to him.

"Please talk to us, Mr. Tamogami. *Tell us what you found in this room and what you did with it.*"

"!"

Shock spread over his face again.

Asuka and Minami also gasped and turned to Musubu.

Does Enoki know *what Tamogami did?*

Tamogami's voice trembled.

"Emon…did he tell you? No, he wouldn't. There's no way he would tell…"

In a heartfelt tone, Musubu continued speaking to him.

"No, he never told anyone. But the books in this room saw what you did. All the books in here are witnesses to your crime."

Tamogami gave a low laugh.

"Ha-ha…the books are witnesses? Are the books taking their revenge on me?"

Minami was sure there was no way he was taking Musubu at his word, but he also must have understood that someone other than Emon was now aware of what he had done, and he figured he could no longer keep it a secret.

"…That's right—in this very room, Emon and his book…I betrayed them both."

Tamogami relayed his story in an anguished voice.

"At the time, I was working as a public servant here in town while submitting my novels to literature contests. No matter how diligently I toiled away, I could never make it past third place—Emon suggested changing the theme of my writing, but I couldn't come up with a good idea for something that would have a broad appeal."

With a faint smile, he recalled how he had discovered a handmade picture book on the shelf of this office.

"The picture book was titled *The Last Bookstore*."

Minami's heart skipped a beat.

The Last Bookstore?! No way!

Asuka seemed as if she must have had a hunch. Her face was frozen in an unhappy grimace.

"In the story, the owner of the one and only bookstore in a small town passes away, and all the townspeople bring their favorite books to the store to hold a funeral."

The plot was practically identical to Tamogami's debut work, *A Funeral for Kanoyama Books*.

"The drawings and prose were simple, but I thought, 'This is it! If I write a story using this plot and setting, it'll definitely captivate the sentimental masses.'"

When he asked Emon about the picture book, the bookseller had admitted bashfully that he'd written the story.

"I wrote it to the best of my ability, but I never planned to show it to anyone. Apparently, I got neither my father's artistic talent nor my grandfather's skill with words."

"His face flushed red, and he seemed truly embarrassed. He wasn't aware of the value of his creation…"

Tamogami looked ashamed.

"At that point, I should have asked Emon to let me use his idea for a book. But I didn't do that. Instead, I used the plot and setting he'd thought up to write my own novel without his permission and submitted it to a contest."

That was the tale of Tamogami's crime and subsequent suffering.
A Funeral for Kanoyama Books, a stolen story, placed first in a literary prize, was published, and became a bestseller.

When he received notice that he had won, Tamogami was horrified. For the first time, he felt the ugliness and the weight of the crime he had committed, and he panicked.

If they published it, Emon would surely read it.

When he did, he would know that Tamogami had plagiarized his story. Emon was sure to hate him for it.

Just imagining Emon's gentle smile stiffening and his kind eyes filling with disappointment and contempt was enough to make Tamogami drop to his knees and tear out his hair.

I just can't stand it!

Besides, what if Emon tells everyone I won the prize with a story I stole from someone else? That would mean utter ruin!

He imagined the stares, the finger pointing, the sneers.

He felt no joy in his victory, only a swell of anxiety.

Do I confide in Emon?

No, I can't tell him.

Do I keep quiet about winning the prize?

If I use a pen name, he won't know it was me who wrote it, right?

No, once he sees the title and the plot, he'll suspect I cribbed it from the story he wrote.

Emon runs a bookstore and is always checking the books that win the new-writer prizes from the major publishers. Even more damning, he knows I've been submitting manuscripts for a while.

No matter how he tried to escape, Emon would inevitably find out.

He would have to confess before the prize winner was announced and apologize.

"But—I couldn't do it."

With his arms crossed tightly across his chest, Tamogami hung his head. His voice was hoarse and shaky.

*   *   *

"Whenever I tried to talk to Emon, my body would stiffen and my throat would ache and start closing up on me, so I couldn't get a word out."

While Tamogami was suffering, the contest results were finally published.
Grand prize goes to Kouichi Tamogami.
The title of his work is A Funeral for Kanoyama Books—
In the commentary, they praised the quality of the setting and the story.
He felt an increasing weight in the pit of his stomach.
At last, the time had come when his ugliness would be exposed.
He feared Emon's denunciation.

"But Emon didn't say anything about the fact that I had stolen his story. He simply said, 'Congratulations, I always knew you would become a great writer one day, Kouichi. I told you ahead of time that I knew you would win, didn't I?' I'm sure I was quiet and standoffish, but I was so shocked… He was smiling gently like always."

Far from reassuring Tamogami, Emon's behavior only increased his suffering.
He must have noticed.
So why doesn't he say anything?
Why doesn't he condemn me?
He's not cursing me for being a thief.
Or maybe, behind that smiling face, he's holding me in contempt?
Maybe he's telling everyone that my prizewinning story is filthy stolen goods?

"It got to the point that I couldn't stand to see Emon's face, so I ran away to a place where I never would.

"I used the prize money to move to Tokyo and started my life there.
"*A Funeral for Kanoyama Books* was published as planned and immediately got a second edition and a movie deal. Everything was going my way.
"But it was all a sham. In my heart, I was always afraid that one day he

would out me as a thief and tell everyone that my book was a sordid piece of plagiarism. The image of Emon's gentle smile never left the back of my mind."

"Congratulations, Tamogami."

"Emon's face from that day surfaced in my mind again and again and again, and I could hear his voice ringing in my ears telling me I had stolen his book. It drove me crazy."

The more *A Funeral for Kanoyama Books* sold, the more Tamogami felt that the evidence of his crime was spreading through the world. He felt as if a huge bird were constantly tearing the flesh off his chest with its enormous beak.

"I tried to contact Emon as little as possible. But when I got the phone call saying he wanted me to come back to hold a book signing at Koumoto Books, he asked me if I remembered our promise, so I couldn't refuse."

"Thank you so much. I'm sure everyone will be thrilled."

Emon had thanked him happily.

Why hasn't he said I stole his book? Well, maybe he couldn't say anything since I escaped to Tokyo.

In that case, is he calling me back to hold a book signing so that he can accuse me now?

Do you suppose he's planning to shame me for my crime in the showiest place possible?

"I was afraid to see him, but there was no avoiding it. On the surface, I was acting like a famous author who had found success in the big city, but underneath all that, I was sure my crime would come to light. I felt dead inside."

Tall stacks of Tamogami's book were piled high in the space that had been set up for the signing on the second floor and in the fiction corner on the first floor.

A Funeral for Kanoyama Books had been used in the design for the promotional materials as well, so the book's cover met the eye no matter where you looked in the shop.

Beneath his suit, Tamogami had broken into a cold sweat. The hand that held his signing pen was cold, and his neck was stiff the whole time.

When is Emon going to say it?

When is that peacefully smiling face going to heap scorn on me?

When will he announce to everyone that the man sitting here is a disgraceful imposter?

"But Emon didn't say a thing."

The whole time the book signing was going on, Emon had attended to Tamogami with a smile on his face, listening to people's compliments for Tamogami as happily as if they were his own.

"That was just—too much to bear!"

He shouted in a sudden outburst.

His eyes were bloodshot, his throat was dry, and he was shaking.

Reverend Dimmesdale in *The Scarlet Letter* is a devout Puritan. His community respects him for being a chaste and honest person.

And yet, he has an affair with another man's wife, who births a child.

The community punishes his partner, forcing her to stand in the stocks and to wear the letter *A* as a symbol of the repugnant crime she had committed.

But even as the scarlet *A* is being sewn onto her clothes, she refuses to say a word about the identity of the child's father, and she labors away despite constant humiliation to raise her daughter.

The minister, Dimmesdale, who had initially gotten away unpunished, grows weaker day by day.

He hasn't been judged for his crime.

*   *   *

But Dimmesdale's sentence is in fact even more severe. Whenever he is alone, he whips his own body. He flogs himself over and over again.

Yet even that isn't enough to alleviate his guilt.

In Dimmesdale's eyes, the bright scarlet *A* isn't there to mark the woman who had committed the crime, but to remind him of his own transgressions.

You have sinned.

Yet you wear the robes of a clergyman without shame and continue basking in the reverent gazes of everyone in town.

You filthy villain.

It's as if the crimson letter itself is accusing him. Seeing the woman accompanied by his growing child is like being in hell.

His suffering continues for seven years.

Finally, on the verge of dying of guilt, he climbs up on the stocks and reveals before the public the letter *A* he had carved into his own chest.

Dimmesdale breathes his last and finds salvation in death.

His eyes would never again see the scarlet *A*. He would fear it no longer.

But Tamogami had lived much longer after committing his crime.

For more than twenty years, he had suffered and feared—and despaired.

Even after leaving his hometown and cutting off all communication with his old friend, Emon's gentle smile haunted his mind.

To Tamogami, that clear smile was worse than any amount of anger or contempt. It was his punishment.

So he ran away.

As far as he could—

He ran and ran and kept running.

He didn't take Emon's calls and wrote short, businesslike replies to his e-mails, trying to keep as much distance as possible.

Even when Emon reached out to tell him that he and Yaeko had had a child, Tamogami couldn't feel happy for them. All he could think was *Do I have to send them a present? Emon will probably thank me for it, but maybe I can get away with handling that by e-mail?*

"You're welcome to come and see us if you'd like."

Emon had said that on the phone, but Tamogami had been noncommittal.

"Sure…someday."

When he'd hung up the phone, his hands and face had been cold and stiff, and he had gotten angry when Asuka had innocently mentioned that she wanted to see the baby.

He had answered her in a stern tone of voice. *"It's impossible. I've got deadlines to keep."*

Even when Asuka asked him if something had happened between him and Emon, all he could do was respond stiffly. *"Nothing happened."*

He took in Asuka and made a life with her, the girl who dreamed of finding fame as an actress in the city, because in her he saw a reflection of his painfully arrogant former self. Tamogami hoped that by becoming her mentor, he might be able to somehow alleviate the guilt he harbored toward Emon.

He believed they were kindred spirits, so he wanted Asuka to pursue her dreams without being tainted by sin.

However, she never really blossomed. In time, she was beset by anxiety, until she only reminded Tamogami of the days he'd spent raging about his failure to make it past third place. In the end, he couldn't help Asuka, and they had a falling out.

Things became uncomfortable after the matter of Emon's baby, and she left his apartment. As she walked out, she said something to him with a miserable look on her face.

"When I'm with you, I feel unsettled, and it's rapidly getting worse."

With Asuka gone, he started thinking about Emon more and more, and from there, his suffering only grew.

As for his work, he was periodically completing commissions, but none of them were able to surpass the sales of this debut work, *A Funeral for Kanoyama Books*. Whenever he heard an editor or a reader ask, *"Please write something like* Kanoyama Books *again,"* it was as if his heart were being gouged out.

Emon's gentle smile would float up in the back of his mind, and Tamogami would hold his head in his hands in his frigid, lonely room, repeating his supplications for forgiveness.

"By that point, it was clear Emon had no intention of telling anyone what I had done. For that very reason, I couldn't stop ruminating about him, which was driving me mad. I was in hell."

Minami, Asuka, and Musubu all stared at Tamogami with stiff faces as he told his tale, sighing with distress as he spoke.

"The afternoon before the day Emon died, he suddenly called me on the phone. My heart nearly stopped—we hadn't had any contact in the nearly ten years since his child was born, so why was he calling me out of the blue?"

"I was looking at a photo from back when you did your book signing, and it got me feeling nostalgic. I wondered how you were doing, Kouichi.

"That was really something—the line went all the way out the building! Everybody had a copy of your book in their hands, and they were all smiling happily.

"Are you sure you won't be coming back here, Kouichi? I'd like to talk about books with you again."

"I'm sure Emon *really did think that*. I'm sure he felt nostalgic and wanted to meet up to talk—but that was impossible for me. When I heard his voice through the phone after more than ten years, it was like a storm began to rage inside my heart, and I—I blurted everything out."

*   *   *

"I don't want to see you…

"Why haven't you told anyone that I'm a criminal who stole your story?

"For over twenty years…you've been smiling, never condemning me, and it's killing me.

"As long as you're alive, I'll never find peace…! I'll always be in hell!"

On the other end of the phone, Emon had been silent.
He had probably been shocked and couldn't say anything.
Just one single phrase got out.

"I'm sorry."

He apologized.
To Tamogami.
In a voice filled with sorrow.

Why?! Why are you apologizing?!
I'm the one who did something cruel to you!
His pitiful apology just gouged at Tamogami's heart even more. He hung up the phone and threw it at the floor.

The very next day, Emon had been arranging books in the shop alone in the middle of the night when he'd slipped off his stepladder. Books had fallen on his head, and he'd died.
Then the day after that—

—a package had come for Tamogami from Emon.
Inside the A4-size envelope was the handmade picture book Tamogami had seen in the office of Koumoto Books all those years ago.

*   *   *

The Last Bookstore.

The moment he saw the title written in crayon, the blood rushed to his head and a sharp pain ran through his chest, as though his heart were being crushed.

Just how much will the virtuous Emon Koumoto have to torment me before he's satisfied?

Did he think it would bring me peace of mind if he offered me the very work I stole?

Preposterous!

He's only increased my suffering!

Tamogami loathed seeing the evidence of his crime.

He thought about throwing it away, but he couldn't bring himself to do it. Instead, he shoved it into the back of his bookshelf and laughed, at his wit's end.

He wondered if he had finally lost his mind.

In a way, that would probably have been easier.

However, an even greater hell was awaiting Tamogami.

News of *Emon Koumoto's death* reached him.

"As long as you're alive, I'll never find peace…" The day after Tamogami said those words, Emon had died in an unfortunate accident.

"I'm sorry."

Emon's pitiful voice reverberated through his mind. Tamogami's whole world had come unmoored.

Was it really an accident?

That you died right after I told you I could never be at ease while you were alive?

"—That man, Emon Koumoto, *he died because of me*, didn't he?"

With a twisted expression on his face, in a voice as if he were spitting up bitter blood, Tamogami begged Minami and the others.

His shoulders slumped, and he hung his head deeply. "Please let me die. I can't take anymore."

Asuka, who had once been his lover, made a pained face. Tears filled her eyes as she held his head to her breast in an embrace. But that wasn't enough to save him.

"Let me die. If I had died earlier, Emon wouldn't have. I'm sure of it. I killed Emon."

He continued mumbling that they should let him die.

In the gray room filled with the smell of death, Minami had been listening to Tamogami's confession, squeezing her left wrist so hard with her right hand that it threatened to leave a bruise.

That was when her lips trembled, and furious words surged out of her.

"That's enough! The boss would absolutely never have taken his own life!"

Book
4

The Faint
Yet Definite
Effect of *Alain*
on *Happiness*

When she was in middle school, Minami had been a very timid girl.

In bed at night, she would be startled awake whenever she heard a sound from the room next door or from upstairs and would lie there straining her ears to hear whatever small thing was rapping or rattling around, praying it would go away soon. She wouldn't sleep a wink.

Whenever an earthquake happened, she worried that the sounds were from aftershocks that would signal another, larger earthquake. It would collapse the apartment building where Minami, her father, her mother, and her little brother lived, trapping them in rubble and killing them. At night, she would sneak around unlocking all the windows in the apartment.

After she did that, she would worry that a robber was going to come in during the middle of the night with a carving knife, and she would tremble until morning with her blanket over her head.

Drops of rain falling on her face whenever she was walking outside terrified her; she feared that some awful disease had infected her and that her skin was going to melt off, so she carried an umbrella even on sunny days.

Whenever someone shouted in a loud voice nearby, she felt as if she was being scolded and would shrink back and start shaking.

Once when a small mole had appeared on her arm, her whole body froze out of fear that it was some serious skin disease, so she read every book about skin ailments that she could find.

When she cut her finger with a kitchen knife while teaching herself to cook, she was plagued by nightmares of getting tetanus and needing to have her arm amputated. She was sure that a persistent cough signaled a disorder of the lungs and again read every medical book she could get her hands on. When her eyes hurt and she noticed small bits of dust dancing in the sunlight, she immediately suspected retinal detachment and ran to the bookstore near the station to look up information on the condition.

When a blister on her tongue was taking a long time to heal, she suspected serious illness of the tongue. When she felt a lump in her breast, she palpated it again and again to check, and when she felt a constant pressure deep in her chest, she was sure it was heart disease and once again searched for information at the bookstore.

Minami's imagination would run wild whenever something went wrong with a part of her body, and she couldn't help but bolt to the bookstore to look up whatever was scaring her. At the time, Minami was also sleep-deprived, had no appetite, and was nearly always suffering from some kind of health problem, so her days were filled with anxiety.

It had all started when a serious earthquake had struck the region where Minami lived with her family. But a year had passed since the earthquake, and all the other children seemed to be living their lives happily just like before.

Only Minami was still worrying over trivial matters and buying up all the volumes she could find in the store about illness—which was yet another thing that worried her.

I'm weird. When will I be all right? Will I be like this forever?

Minami made her purchases at Koumoto Books, near the train station.

There had been a small bookseller about ten minutes from her house, but it had closed after the earthquake. Now there was a convenience store standing there.

Many other stores besides that one had also closed after the earthquake.

In those days, she worried that everyone would move away and the town would be left empty.

Won't Koumoto Books close, too?

If it does, where will I be able to buy books? I don't have a credit card to shop online, so I would have to ask my parents, and I can't do that.

The library makes you wait your turn for new books, so it's hard to borrow them. Besides, libraries around here aren't likely to even have the sorts of books

I want, with the newest information on different diseases. And of course, the library at school won't have them, either.

If Koumoto Books disappears, I won't be able to research illnesses.

Whenever Minami anxiously pushed open the door of the slim three-story building sandwiched between other various-use buildings, she would see the place bustling with customers and feel relieved that the store didn't seem to be in danger of closing any time soon.

And the kind-looking man with glasses who wore an apron with the store's name on it was always there behind the register on the first floor, greeting customers with a gentle smile.

"Welcome!"

There seemed to be a lot of customers who came just to talk to him. "Emon," they called him. From old people down to small children—he answered them all with a bright smile.

He was apparently the owner of the shop.

When Minami entered the store, he smiled at her just as he did the other customers, but she would cast her pimple-covered face down and stagger past the register to the place where the books on disease were kept.

After spending two or three hours there, she would purchase a single volume on her way out.

The books she bought were more expensive than comic books or paperbacks, and Minami's monthly allowance didn't come close to covering the cost. That's why she would use the extra cash she'd earned helping her mother and the money she'd saved from holidays.

One day, her stomach was feeling upset, and she thought it was probably some sort of stomach disorder, so she flipped through every page of a book that had the name of a familiar disease written on the cover.

Whenever Minami thought something was wrong with her body, she felt compelled to look up every illness she could think of. She could only relax once she'd confirmed that she didn't have any of those illnesses.

But the more she searched, the more she read about symptoms that seemed to match her own, so she just got more worried.

She felt a sharp pain in her chest when that happened, as if someone were crushing her with both hands, and it got hard to breathe.

It hurts.

I can't stand it.

So I really am sick.
I'm going to die.

I hate this.
I'm scared.

Still grasping the medical book in both hands, she squeezed her eyes tightly shut, hung her head, and clenched her teeth—

"Miss, are you not feeling well?"

The shop owner with the glasses addressed her, worried.

He invited her to rest awhile in the back, and she followed him up to the second-floor office since she was suffering too badly that day to turn him down.

Enclosed by gray concrete, the room contained a shelf lined with a variety of books and a mysterious painting hanging on the wall.

The painting depicted a blue ocean and a gray shore where pure-white bird bones stood upright like tombstones. It was desolate—and a little scary.

She sat on the sofa, staring up at it with a drawn face.

"My father painted that. He passed away, but he used to own this shop," he told her as he came back into the room holding cups full of tea. *"It's titled* Extinction.*"*

"...Extinction?"

The sound of it gave her the chills, and she unconsciously wrapped her arms around her body. The shop owner handed her a cup of hot tea.

Minami timidly brought it to her mouth.

It's sweet…

Roasted tea?

It was a calming flavor.

It wasn't too hot or too cold. It had been prepared at just the right temperature, and Minami felt her frigid body slowly start to warm up.

"You come here often to buy books, don't you, miss? It seems like a lot of them are in the medical field. Are you interested in a career in health care?"

He probably brought the subject up in that way so it would be easy for Minami to talk about. Emon had already anticipated the reason why Minami only ever bought books like that. That was why he had invited Minami into this room.

Minami shrunk in on herself and answered with embarrassment.

"No…um… I feel bad a lot, and when I do, I worry that it's something serious, so I just come to look stuff up in books."

"Is that so? Have the books you've purchased been any help?"

"…I don't know."

She couldn't give him a real answer. Minami seemed to shrink even further.

No matter how many books she bought, eventually she would fixate on some other ailment, and she would run for the bookstore.

Over and over again.

Living itself is scary, scary, scary. And unbearably stressful—

Had the huge number of books piled up in Minami's room actually ever helped her? Had they *cured* her?

The answer to that was definitely *no*.

"Well then, how about I give you some medicine today?"

The store owner gave her a gentle smile, then pulled a book off the shelf and held it out to Minami.

The cover had an image of a child-sized angel with wings sprouting from its back, drawn in a calm, airy, pale color palette. It was a fairly thick book.

"Alain on Happiness…?"

* * *

Minami was perplexed, but the store owner smiled reassuringly and narrowed his eyes behind his glasses, then continued speaking.

"I like Alain's writing on happiness, and I've read various translations, but I thought this one was the easiest to understand and made the most sense. So please give it a try if you'd like."

"Um...money?"

"No need. This is my own personal copy."

"But—"

"Look, if you read it, I'd like to hear your thoughts. It doesn't have to be all at once. It's broken up into small chapters, so it's fun to pick out titles that appeal to you and read those." Emon grinned.

Minami thanked him and accepted the gift, then she left the store without buying the book on stomach ailments and went home carrying only the book he'd given her.

In her room, she sat down at her desk and opened the cover. There were ninety-three headings in all.

"The Famous Horse Bucephalus"

"Sad Mary"

"Depression, the Pest"

"On Death"

"How to Yawn"

"Sullenness"

"Prophetic Souls"

"The Happy Farmer"

*   *   *

"On Despair"

"In the Rain"

"Disentangling"

"One Remedy"

"Spiritual Hygiene"

Those were some of the titles. And then there were the final five.

"Happiness Is a Virtue"

"Happiness Is a Generous Thing"

"Methods for Becoming Happy"

"The Obligation to Become Happy"

"Swear an Oath"

It was a succession of headings that each had to do with happiness.

She started by looking over the first entry, "The Famous Horse Bucephalus."

It used an anecdote about Alexander the Great as an example. In his younger days, he was presented with a famous horse named Bucephalus. No trainer had been able to tame the unbreakable stallion.

But Alexander realized Bucephalus was in fact terrified of his own shadow.

He would leap with fright, and his shadow would jump with him, which would frighten him again and cause him to thrash about, and the cycle would go on forever.

Seeing this, Alexander stepped in and pointed Bucephalus's muzzle toward the sun, calming the horse.

"Many people have argued that what we call fear has no basis in reality. They have offered varied and reasonable proofs for this assertion. However, the fearful man does not incline his ear to reason. He listens only to the pounding of his heart and the rushing of his blood."

I see... So I'm like Bucephalus...
These words came readily to Minami's mind.
They gave her a strange sensation.
It felt as if the words were a small pill that slid smoothly down her throat and fell into her stomach, where it dissolved and spread out into every corner of her body, permeating her completely.
There must be a real reason for my fear, like how Bucephalus struggled violently when he saw his own shadow.
And like how Alexander calmed the horse by turning his muzzle toward the sun, if Minami could no longer see her shadow, there would be nothing to be scared about.
There is a reason for this thing called "fear."
Knowing that reason is essential.
Minami came to this conclusion, then carefully continued reading section by section, one at a time, turning each over in her mind.

"The reason why a person is happy or unhappy is not very important. All reasons are dependent on the workings of the body. And no matter how healthy a man may be, every day he is shifting from mental strain to depression, or from depression to mental strain. Moreover, in many cases, the shift is brought about by food, or a walk, or attentiveness, or reading, or the state of the weather."

As Minami read that passage, she heaved a sigh of relief.
Is that so...? It was normal for people to feel bad a hundred years ago, too...
Weather, food, and other minor stuff in everyday life can change your feelings and your health, and that's all it is...

Under the heading "Medicine" were many revelatory passages.

"First and most importantly, it is essential to feel as contented as possible. Secondly, it is necessary to dispel any worries concerning the physical body, as well as those worries that disturb the equilibrium of living."

"In the history of every nation, we can see people who died because they were convinced that they had been cursed. So can we not say that curses are extremely successful, so long as the person in question has been informed that he is cursed?"

"That is to say, nearly all illnesses are nothing but creations of one's own cautions and worries, and it follows that the most reliable method of treatment is to fear stomach ailments or kidney disease no more than one would fear a blister on the foot."

A curse has no effect if the cursed person does not realize they are cursed.
The important thing is not to be afraid.
Not to curse myself by being overcautious.
Ah, I see now.
I was laying a curse on myself. I have to stop doing that.

On the first page after opening the cover was a picture of the author, Alain, a kind and gentle-looking man with an impressive nose.

Minami thought he slightly resembled the owner of Koumoto Books. The whole time she was reading, she imagined she could hear his mellow, kind voice speaking to her.

In the book, the topic of yawning comes up repeatedly, and the author explains that yawns are extremely effective against the illnesses that the imagination invents.

"Humans can stretch our bodies and yawn at will. This is the best exercise to combat anxiety and fretfulness."

*   *   *

"If you yawn, it stops hiccups. But how should one yawn on command? First, start by stretching the body and pretending to yawn. With any luck, miming a yawn will cause a true yawn to come out."

"I believe that yawns, just like the sleep that they precede, are most effective against all sorts of ailments. And that is the proof that our thinking is always closely connected to our physical well-being."

While she was reading enthusiastically, Minami got sleepy and really did let out a yawn.

Sitting in her chair, raising her arms and stretching them upward while looking up and opening her mouth wide to yawn was an incredibly refreshing action. It felt absolutely great.

After that, Minami continued reading *Alain on Happiness* bit by bit every day.

The book seemed to have been written especially for her. There were parts she agreed with, parts that encouraged her, and lots of parts that made her realize things. Just as the owner of Koumoto Books had said, it was the gentle medicine that Minami's heart had desperately needed.

"Right now, as I am writing this, it is raining. The roof tiles are making noise, the murmur of countless tiny grooves. The air seems to have been washed clean, as if put through a filter. The clouds resemble magnificent puffs of cotton.

"We must learn to perceive this kind of beauty.

"Some people say that the rain spoils the harvest. Others say that it gets everything filthy with mud. Still others complain that it ruins the pleasure of sitting in the grass.

"All of this goes without saying. Everyone knows these things. But complaining about them won't do any good.

* * *

"And should I get soaked in the rain of discontent, that rain will follow me into my home.

"Especially when it is raining, we want to see bright and cheerful faces. For that reason, whenever the weather is bad, one must wear a happy face."

Smile cheerfully, especially on rainy days!
Find the beauty in life, especially because it's a rainy day!

As she told herself this, the fog that had been hanging over Minami's head seemed to clear away.

A passage in the section with the heading "Optimism" became her new guiding principle.

"If you think that you are going to collapse, then you will. If you think that you cannot do anything, then you cannot. If you think that you will be betrayed by your expectations, then you will be.

"We produce our own weather, our own storms. First and most importantly, create your own interior atmosphere. Then you can influence your surroundings and the rest of the human world."

So even if I'm in the middle of a raging storm, if it's clear inside my mind, there will be clear skies.
First, I have to raise the sun in the sky of my mind.
I have to believe, with clear and sunny thoughts, that I am capable.

The owner of Koumoto Books had prescribed Minami just the remedy she'd needed. She wasn't as fearful of small irregularities in her body as she had been before, and she started sleeping soundly through the night.

Her pale, pimply skin turned a rosy pink, and it felt smooth when she stroked it with both hands while washing her face in the morning.

Her posture improved, and her eyes, which had been bloodshot from lack of sleep, sparkled. The weight lifted from her once-heavy eyelids, and her vision cleared.

She still visited Koumoto Books as often as she had before, but not to purchase medical books. Now she went to chat with the owner.

Emon always listened to Minami with a kind look in his eye and would elicit more and more comments from her.

Once Minami had finished reading *Alain on Happiness*, he introduced her to other books, which she purchased and read at home. Whenever she finished reading one, she would excitedly go visit Koumoto Books.

Her favorite book, the one that was most special to her, was of course *Alain on Happiness*, which Emon had initially chosen for her. She would reread it at night before bed until she had completely memorized her favorite passages.

And then Minami had her greatest stroke of good luck in her second year of high school.

She shook with joy when she saw the HELP WANTED notice posted on the wall of Koumoto Books.

She immediately went to find the owner, walking around in a daze until she came upon him sorting books in the children's reading corner on the second floor and ran up to him.

"Please allow me to work here!"

She had hardly glanced at the hourly wage and other conditions.

Ever since Emon had prescribed *Alain on Happiness* to her, Minami had held hope in her heart that she could work with him at Koumoto Books one day. She intended to make that wish reality.

She probably would have offered to help even if it were a volunteer position that didn't pay at all.

Emon's eyes rounded behind his glasses, then he smiled gently.

"Mmm, well, I suppose I'll take you up on that."

"All right! I'll do my best!"

*   *   *

"You'll have to make sure to get your parents' permission. You're still in high school, Minami, so you can't neglect your studies."

"I'll be fine! I'm so happy right now, I feel like I can do anything!"

And that's how Minami started working at Koumoto Books.

Each day brought happiness, and she enjoyed her job.

Her heart fluttered every time she carefully opened heavy cardboard boxes with a box cutter to reveal the brand-new books packed inside. Taking them out to arrange them on the flatbed displays, thinking about what layout would most appeal to the customers and how best to grab their attention thrilled her.

Her heart would pound when she saw the excitement of other high schoolers who had come to buy books.

"All right! It's here! See, I told you Koumoto Books would have it."

"I bought a book I saw on display here, and it turned out to be really interesting!"

Her heart seemed as if it would soar up to heaven when customers said those things.

She even came to appreciate the painting titled *Extinction* that decorated the office wall. When she had first laid eyes on it, she had trembled with fear, but she eventually became quite fond of the piece after seeing it every day at work.

Moreover, she came to consider it achingly beautiful.

"Your father's painting is lovely, isn't it?"

Emon's eyes narrowed in a smile as he answered.

"Yeah, I think so, too."

.

*   *   *

Happiness filled every corner of her body when she heard that her and Emon's thoughts on the painting were in alignment.

"My grandfather was an aspiring writer, and my father wanted to be an artist or an actor, you know. Both of them died young and didn't get their wish, though."

"What did you dream of being when you were little, boss?"

When Minami asked that, he answered with a dazzling smile.

"I always wanted to run a bookstore."

He explained that for as long as he could remember, he had been surrounded by books and been hopelessly in love them, so he had always wanted to help connect people to them.

Emon would always talk like that, and Minami would listen with a sweet feeling inside.

Even after Minami graduated and enrolled at a local university, she continued working her part-time job at Koumoto Books. When it came time for her to look for work, Emon offered to help.

"If you're job hunting in the area, some of our customers run their own companies or are in charge of hiring. Would you like me to talk to them?"

But Minami had stopped him.

"No, I'll keep working here even after I graduate."

"Thank you, but…no matter how great you are, Minami, we don't have room in the budget to hire you as a full-time employee."

He'd looked somewhat stumped.

However—

"I'm commuting from home as it is, so I'll make it work. Besides, I've been thinking of getting certified as a tax accountant, so I want to be able to study for that."

She had added the part about becoming a tax accountant so that she wouldn't make him worry and so that he would allow her to continue her part-time job at Koumoto Books even after graduating from college.

"Feel free to quit any time you like, okay? I'm also not sure how much longer we'll be around."

They had been losing ground to e-books and online shopping, and sales had been dropping steadily. Koumoto Books was already the last bookstore in town.

And Emon had no successor.

His wife and child had died in the earthquake, Minami had heard.

The elderly part-timer who had told Minami the story had been moved to tears.

"Emon's son was named Mirai. He was just six years old—the cutest little thing.

"His wife, Yaeko, miscarried their first child, and apparently the doctor told her she couldn't have children anymore. So when little Mirai was born, they were truly overjoyed. To think that it ended in tragedy."

Mirai loved books, and he would always sit down quietly on the mat in the children's section happily reading. He looked exactly like Emon had when he was young.

"He would tell you in his cute voice, 'I'm going to run a bookstore, too, just like Papa!' ...Emon would melt when he heard it. Really, why did such a horrible thing happen to such a sweet boy?

*   *   *

Naming the child they had been miraculously blessed with Mirai—meaning "future"—Emon must have been imagining the continuing legacy of Koumoto Books.

He was the third owner, and after he passed away, there would be a fourth owner, and a fifth, and a sixth… On and on it would continue. He must have wished for his family to continue connecting people and books right there.

And yet, the earthquake had stolen away both futures too soon.

Despite the tragedy, Emon smiled kindly when he spoke.

"As long as I am alive, I'm keeping the store going. If we closed, many of our customers would be disappointed, you see."

It seemed as though he'd always known that sooner or later, all the bookstores would disappear from town.

Minami could tell he was serious about believing that he had a duty to perform, and he did it earnestly, without regret or fear and without holding on to any kind of resentment.

He would simply work solemnly until his final day arrived.

And Minami wanted to be by his side.

She wondered if what she was feeling was love.

Her heart pounded excitedly whenever he smiled at her. She felt happy and proud whenever he called her by name, and it made her wish he would open up to her.

Working at Koumoto Books, she had learned of Emon's secret sorrow and suffering. And she had also seen how, despite all that, he smiled gently and lived honestly. His quiet love for books and people, plus everything else about him, was just like the writings in *Alain on Happiness*, the book he had prescribed for Minami.

She used him as a model for life—the way he lived, the words he spoke, his strength in hiding his pain behind a smile, his kindness, his love for others.

Was it love?

Or was it something stronger that only resembled love?

Minami didn't know.

But she wanted to be by his side forever if she could, to protect both Koumoto Books and its owner with all her strength.

She hadn't wanted to think about it coming to an end.

◇   ◇   ◇

"The boss would absolutely never have taken his own life!"

With complete devotion, Minami shouted at Tamogami, who was now reclining on the sofa, holding his head in his hands.

He had been weeping about how he had caused Emon's death, and he was obviously very upset. But Minami knew there was no way the boss had done something so stupid.

"Even if the novel you wrote using the boss's ideas did become a big bestseller, the fact that he never said anything about it means he cared about your feelings. It certainly wasn't something he would have held a grudge about! If anything, he was probably happy you got famous with a book that borrowed his ideas! The Emon Koumoto I knew—my boss—that's the kind of person he was!"

Tamogami, Asuka, and the glasses-wearing high schooler to whom Emon had entrusted the store's books were all staring at her.

Tamogami looked distressed, Asuka looked sad, and Musubu was just gazing quietly with clear eyes—

Behind Musubu hung the painting of bird bones discarded by the seashore.

That quiet, lonely, beautiful picture.

"After the earthquake, I turned into a real scaredy-cat. Every day, I would imagine some new thing to be afraid of, and my fear would follow me everywhere, until living itself became an utter nightmare. I was always shaking, wondering what horrible thing would happen tomorrow. That's what I was like when Emon prescribed me the medicine of Alain's *Alain on Happiness*! He told me he loved the book so much that he'd read many different translations!"

On the office bookshelf stood five translations of *Alain on Happiness*, each different from the one Minami had.

Emon had always read the books on his shelf during breaks or when he was working a night shift. He had certainly read *Alain on Happiness* many times over.

"This book teaches how to resist worrying about imagined ailments and methods for turning rainy days into sunny ones—ways to become happy! There are lots of them written here! The power of imagination will never make us happy! Imagination cannot create anything. Creation comes through action! Thinking you are naturally just a certain way and nothing can change that is like placing a curse on yourself! The grief you get from obsessing about the past is worse than useless—it's poisonous! Dwelling in regret is the same as repeating the mistake! You have to punch back at the real source of your sorrow!"

She shouted desperately, until her throat was raw.

Just as the words written in *Alain on Happiness* had encouraged Minami, so, too, must have Emon taken it off the shelf to read whenever he was feeling disheartened or assaulted by sadness.

By doing that, he would have hit back at the sadness and smiled.

He narrowed his eyes gently and kindly.

You always smiled through thick and thin, just like the first time you served me tea in this office!

"If you don't want to become happy, you never will! You have to wish for happiness of your own and make it come true!"

The Emon that Minami knew had lived his life that way.

"There's no chance a person who would recommend a book like that would ever take his own life!"

Tamogami frowned and stubbornly gritted his teeth as he listened to Minami's speech. Over and over, despair, denial, and doubt passed across his face, which was lined with exhaustion and suffering.

But Emon did die.

He died the day after I said those cruel things to him.

Died after sending me that handmade picture book.

Tamogami felt as if he might shout these words from his trembling lips at any moment.

Just then, a clear voice rang out.

"It's as Minami says."

They all turned to see the high school boy with large glasses—Musubu Enoki had spoken with a gentle expression that almost made them believe he was Emon.

With the painting of the bird bones on the beach titled *Extinction* at his back, he continued with a look of quiet wisdom in his eyes that took everyone's breath away.

"Emon did not kill himself. I know the real cause of his death. And I'll reveal it to you now."

Final Book

My Encounter with *The Long, Long Story of the Postman*

I first became acquainted with Emon Koumoto at the end of a long summer, when the cool breezes of autumn had just begun to blow.

It was a holiday the day we met. I was sitting on a bench in a park that was fragrant with the scent of sweet olive trees, soaking in the beautiful sunshine, chatting to my *girlfriend* with a pale-colored book on my knee.

"Whenever I smell sweet olive, I feel like it's already autumn. Princess Yonaga, you can hear people's voices, but can you smell things, too?"

"Sorry, sorry, I wasn't trying to make fun of you!"

"I see—so you burn incense. I guess you are a princess after all."

"Huh? The Ten Virtues of the Incense-Smelling Ceremony? By Huang Tingjian? A Chinese poet, was he? Hmm...never heard of it."

"Wow, so when you smell the incense, your senses get keener, like a demon or a god..."

"'Befriend the quiet'... That means you come to feel as if the silence is your friend, right? You sure know a lot of things, Princess."

*   *   *

"No, I'm not saying you're old! You're not antique or worn-out, not in the slightest."

"I mean it! I've read you many times, and I love your soft, slightly yellowed, easy-to-read pages. The fact that your cover is a little bit faded gives you character and makes me feel like you're my book."

"No, wait, when I say that you're yellowed, it's so minor that you can't even tell unless you put your face right up close. It's not like you're bright yellow or anything."

"Yes, yes, even after fifty years or a hundred, you'll always be beautiful and cute!"

"Huh? I can turn your pages here? But you always say I can't because you don't want to turn brown in the sunlight."

"No, I always want to turn your pages, I always want to read you, but—are you sure it's okay, even though you really hate the sun?"

"No, no, I'm very happy, thank you."

"All right, I'll hold you in the shade so the sun won't hit you, okay?"

I was flirting with my cute girlfriend, taking advantage of the fact that there was no one around. That day, my usually cold girlfriend was letting me enjoy a little taste of her precious affection.

So there I was, appreciating our autumn date among the fragrant sweet olive trees, when the crunchy sound of someone stepping on a fallen leaf came from behind me.

When I turned to look, there was a man with glasses standing behind the bench, his eyes wide.

Ah, there was someone here.

*   *   *

I had been too absorbed in listening to Princess Yonaga's chilly, cherubic, charming voice to notice.

The man had undoubtedly heard me talking.

I had just been enjoying a simple date with my girlfriend, but unfortunately, other people can't hear the voices of books, which I often take for granted. Because of that, I probably looked as if I had been talking to myself on a park bench like some kind of crazy person.

Ah, I messed up.

At school, I was already known as something of an eccentric character, so even if I did get caught talking to a book, everyone would just tease me about it. "Enoki's going crazy again!" "How about reading a light novel or something normal?" "Your little wife is gonna curse you again!" Outside of school, I tried my best not to talk to any books in front of people.

Maybe he thinks I'm creepy?

No, he looks like a nice person, so maybe he's worried about me. He's probably going to ask me if I'm in trouble or something.

Well, that's a common mistake people make about me, so I'll just laugh it off like I usually do.

But the man didn't ask me if I was in trouble or who I had been talking to.

With a very surprised look on his face, he said something unexpected.

"Are you *able to talk to books,* too, *by any chance?"*

That was the first time I had ever been asked that question.

Too, he had said.

In other words, the man staring at me with wide eyes through the lenses of his glasses could also talk to books.

"Yeah, can you *hear the voices of books, too?!"*

I was too excited. I answered a question with a question.

The man smiled happily as he replied.

*   *   *

"No. I can sort of understand them somehow, but I can't hear their words clearly. But you can, right? You can hear her voice."

With deep kindness in his eyes, he gazed at the slim book with the light-blue cover that I was holding in my hands. A person who looks at books like that is someone who loves them from the bottom of their heart. I could tell he was definitely a good person!

"Yes, I can! She's my girlfriend, Princess Yonaga. When we're alone together, I usually talk to her like I was just now. My name is Musubu Enoki. I'm a first-year at a high school nearby."

I introduced myself, and the man made an even kinder, friendlier face.

"I'm Emon Koumoto. I'm here for work."

Emon told me he ran a bookstore in a small town in Tohoku and in fact was the owner of the place.

"A bookseller? That's awesome! The books that line the shelves in stores are very chatty and lively, you know. Especially the new releases on the flat displays. They all call out like little newborn chicks, 'Read me! Read me!'"

"Yeah, I know. Doesn't matter what kind, the freshly delivered new releases are always very excited, huh? I get the sense they just can't wait to be read. Whenever I open one of their covers, I can practically feel their exuberance."

"That's right! That's it exactly! Books that have just gone on sale are like little kids full of curiosity. They wait for someone who will read them, and they get really happy and attached to anyone who picks them up. They're so cute, right? Wah! Princess Yonaga, n-no, you've got it wrong; I'm not talking about cheating! I just think they're innocent and cute. It's a totally different kind of 'cute' than when I talk about you! I'm sorry—don't curse me."

*   *   *

I apologized frantically to her as she was making accusations in that frigid voice of hers, and Emon watched me with a smile.

"I'm sorry, my girlfriend is the jealous type. She hates it when I talk about other books."

"That sounds rough. I'm sure she's very devoted to you. And very proud. Her name seems very appropriate."

"Yes, she's my precious princess."

Princess Yonaga's mood seemed to improve as I had this exchange with Emon. After all, as a book herself, she couldn't help but be fond of someone who spoke about books with such a kind expression like he did.

After that, he and I sat on the bench together and talked for quite a long time.

"Emon, you said you understand how books are feeling, but what form does that take? Like, do the books sparkle with happiness or something?"

"No, it's really more like a feeling, like, 'Oh, that one seems happy'...or 'That one seems lonely'... I'm probably just imagining it most of the time. I often wish I could hear their voices and have conversations with them like you can, Musubu."

Emon smiled and continued.

"Oh, but there is one way! Whenever I lay my palm over the cover of a book... My palm gets very warm if it's happy."

"Your palm?"

"Yes, and the opposite is also true. If the book is feeling sad, my palm gets cold."

*   *   *

I placed my palm flat against Princess Yonaga's cover.

She grew mad at me, chiding me for suddenly touching her with my sweaty hand and told me to touch her gently only after I had washed my hands properly with soap. The tone of her voice sounded a little bashful. It was cute.

But she didn't feel particularly warm or cold.

"Hmm…guess I can't feel it. But that's really amazing. Even if you can't hear their words, you can tell how a book's feeling just by touching it. How long have you been able to do that? I've apparently been able to hear them ever since I was born.

"According to my sister, I would babble at books as a baby, which she thought was weird. To be fair, my older sister, who is now attending medical school in Hokkaido, always did have a sharp tongue…"

"I suppose I've also been able to do it since childhood. My father was the second-generation owner of the bookshop, and my mother passed away soon after she gave birth to me, so Dad used to take me with him to work. I was basically raised in the bookstore. There were lots of books around, and it was always a mystery to me why, when I touched them, some felt warm and others felt cold."

He told me that when he was ten years old, he had an encounter with a particular book.

"It was an anthology of works by Karel Čapek called The Long, Long Story of the Postman. *In the title story, there are some little magical people. They come out to help the postman in the middle of the night, and they're able to tell the content of a letter just by touching it, without opening the envelope."*

"When we touch them, the letters filled with blunt, plain writing feel chilly, cold even. But the more emotional sentiment that is included in a letter, the warmer it will feel in the hand.

*   *   *

"Also, just by pressing the letters to our foreheads, we can tell exactly what's written in them, word for word."

A deliveryman for the post office named Kolbaba hears this from the little people, and after that, he, too, starts mumbling to himself while holding letters in his hands.

"This letter is slightly warm, eh? But this letter is much, much warmer. I'm certain that this letter must be one written by a mother to her child."

"—*When I read that, I thought, 'Ah…so that's what it is!' When I touched a book with my palm and it felt warm, that book was happy, and if it felt cold, that book was sad, I realized.*"

Unfortunately, Emon explained, even if he pressed a book cover against his forehead, he couldn't hear the book's exact words. He laughed.

"*If I'm Kolbaba, I guess that must make you one of his little helpers, Musubu. Just as it was fortunate for him to meet the tiny little people, it was my good fortune to make your acquaintance today.*"

"*Yeah! I feel the same way! I'm so happy to meet another person who can understand the feelings of books!*"

We exchanged contact information.

"*Please let me know whenever you come to Tokyo! We can talk about books again!*"

"*—Sure, I will. You, too, come visit my shop sometime and chat with my collection.*"

"*—Wow, I will! I can't wait!*"

*   *   *

After that day, Emon and I kept in touch, and whenever he came to Tokyo, I always made time to see him.

He told me all sorts of things about his life.

He told me about his grandmother, Natsu, who had opened up a bookstore after the war, and his sickly grandfather who had wanted to be a writer. He told me about his father, Kanesada, who had been so skilled at reading aloud and so popular with the children, and about how he had wanted to be an artist or an actor. He even told me about his wife and child who had died in the earthquake…

After that, I heard about his author friend, Mr. Tamogami.

And about the people who worked with him in the shop.

And about how Emon's bookstore was the last one in town.

"Koumoto Books will probably end with my generation.

"Just like all the creatures that have gone extinct and disappeared from the face of the earth, I think books and bookstores are probably undergoing an extinction of their own.

"They're destined for annihilation, unable to survive in their current form…"

Even I was aware of the fact that for the past several years, the number of physical books published had dropped dramatically, while sales of digital publications had been increasing.

Not to mention that fewer and fewer people were even reading books at all.

Whenever I considered the prospect of books disappearing from this world, I would feel so lonesome it was as if a gaping hole had suddenly formed in the middle of my chest.

If that ever happened, so many friends and companions would disappear from my life. It was a frightening prospect.

Emon, who showered his books with deep affection, felt the same.

But he didn't seem depressed as he spoke about it—he was as calm and graceful as ever.

That's the kind of man Emon Koumoto was.

"Of course, I'm sure it will be many years before books change form completely, and I'm going to keep Koumoto Books going as long as I live."

He made that conclusion in a gentle voice.

It was just after the New Year when I unexpectedly received a call from Emon.

Not an e-mail—he went out of his way to call me on the phone. I wondered if it was a New Year's greeting call, perhaps? Or maybe he was coming to Tokyo on business again? When I answered, he quietly confided in me.

"It seems the store will be closing earlier than I thought."

His words were devastating to hear, and he sounded very pained and downcast.

And then, during that phone call, he made a very important request of me.

◇   ◇   ◇

"He'd developed a terminal brain tumor. The doctors estimated he had, at best, six months left to live."

The night was really wearing on. Normally, I would have been falling asleep at that hour, but I was wide awake. And I was certain the other people in the room with me were feeling the same.

Ms. Tsuburaya the part-timer, Mr. Tamogami the author, and Asuka the actress. All three of them were staring at me with disbelief on their faces.

I, too, hadn't believed it when Emon had confided in me. I hadn't wanted to believe it.

He was the first person I had ever met who understood the feelings of books.

An extremely kind person—a gentle man with a beautiful disposition—it was unthinkable someone like him would be robbed from this world in only half a year's time.

"So that's why he entrusted all the titles in Koumoto Books to me in the will he left with his lawyer. His unfortunate accident did mean I had to come here earlier than planned, though."

"The boss had...a brain tumor?" Ms. Tsuburaya muttered, face stiff.

She had idolized Emon and had worked at Koumoto Books for a long time, so she must have felt great shock at the news. My heart ached for her.

But his brain tumor was proof that his death was not a suicide.

"The tumor caused both his fall from the stepladder and his death. He told me he would sometimes get sudden, awful headaches, you see. While he was arranging the books, he must have lost his balance, grabbed for some books, and caused an avalanche as he fell. One of the books happened to hit him in a vital spot, and he struck his head on the corner of the display table while falling, which was the fatal blow—he did not commit suicide. As Ms. Tsuburaya said, Emon Koumoto was not the kind of person who would choose death, not for any reason. It was an unfortunate accident."

"Who killed Emon?"

That had been the answer I had received when I had asked the books. They had been loudly bemoaning that they had slain their beloved caretaker.

"No way... But Emon sent me that picture book, and then..."

Mr. Tamogami wore a grim scowl, as if he were having trouble understanding.

Clearly, he was desperate to bear the responsibility for Emon's death. And he wanted the weight of that crime to drag him down to his own death.

When I had gone searching for him earlier and found him shut up in the bathroom, having slit his own wrist, the books that led me there had all been astir.

"That man means to die!"

"Be careful!"

"He went into the toilets."

"Hurry! Take something with you to open the lock."
"He wants to die."
"He'll die."
"He'll die."
"He'll die."

"When Emon suddenly called Mr. Tamogami out of the blue, it was because he had just gotten his diagnosis from the doctor, and he knew his death was close at hand. So he wanted to see his old friend. His estrangement from Tamogami had always bothered him, and he was hoping they would be able to talk about books again, like old times."

"Mr. Tamogami is an author from our hometown, you know, and he once held a book signing at my shop. The line of customers stretched all the way outside... The people and the books seemed so happy, so cheerful... That is my proudest and most joyful memory."

"...Tch, there's no way he thought of me like that! I stole Emon's story, used it to win a writing competition, and then ran away without even apologizing!" Mr. Tamogami's voice was beginning to crack, and his face contorted with doubt and distress.

How can I possibly convey Emon's heartfelt wishes to him?

"Emon never said anything like that about you to me. From what he told me, he was really proud and happy when you came to Koumoto Books to hold your book signing because you had always worked so seriously on your writing, certain that you would become an author one day, and your dream had come true."

"No way... There's no way..."

"Ms. Tsuburaya said it, too, right? He actually seemed overjoyed that you used his idea to win such a prestigious award. I'm sure he was, too."

"...Oh."

"I'm also sure he worried about you after you started avoiding him out of guilt, but he didn't want to say anything about it. Also, don't you think he sent you the picture book before he died both as a memento and to make sure nobody else would see it after he passed? I'm sure he'd hoped the two of you could talk to each other, like you used to."

How can I possibly repair Emon and Tamogami's relationship when it's so hopelessly twisted and complicated?

What words can I use to ease his feelings when he's so burdened by guilt?

What on earth can I say?

"Stop it, please!"

Mr. Tamogami's scream reverberated around the little gray room.

He shook off Asuka's arms and pitched forward with both hands against the sofa. Eyes wild and breathing heavy, he spoke.

"I'm begging you, please stop. Everything you people have said is just well-meaning speculation! What Emon was really thinking, why he never condemned me for stealing his idea, how he was able to smile at me with a clear face like that—I've thought and thought and thought long and hard about it—and I don't know. I don't know, I don't know! Please tell me, Emon... Emon..."

There was nothing but despair in his voice and on his face.

My words could not get through to him as he was now. He wasn't going to believe anything besides Emon's own words. But Emon wasn't here anymore.

Tamogami kept calling for him anyway.

"Emon, Emon!"

Just then, my ears picked up a faint voice.

"Kouichi?"

A voice like a small child...
From where?

"That's not true, Kouichi!"

The sweet little voice called out to him with all its might.

"Neither Papa nor I were ever mad at you!"

* * *

I held my breath and strained my ears.

The voice was coming from the blue storage box under the breathtaking painting titled *Extinction*.

The same box that had held the picture book *The Field Guide of Extinct Animals*.

"Read me, Kouichi!

"If you read me, I can communicate my papa's words to you, Kouichi."

The youthful voice continued speaking courageously—

I fixed my gaze on Tamogami and asked, "If you think my words are just speculation, then how about we talk to *Emon himself*?"

His face twisted as if he was puzzled by what I was saying.

Asuka and Ms. Tsuburaya also looked baffled.

I turned my back on them, crouched down on the floor, and opened the blue box.

The owner of the voice was staring back at me from inside.

It was a picture book with a cardboard cover, on which *The Last Bookstore* was written in blue crayon, the only one of its kind in the world.

So it was you.

Will you help me out?

Speaking to the book in my mind, I gently lifted the slim, handmade volume out of the box with both hands.

"Enoki, is that…? It can't be!" Ms. Tsuburaya shouted.

The "child" that Emon had created thanked me for finding it as it sat atop my open hands.

"But I thought the boss sent that to Mr. Tamogami—," Ms. Tsuburaya mumbled as she looked down at the picture book. Asuka was regarding Tamogami with confusion in her eyes.

He looked surprised that I had pulled Emon's book from the box.

"And you returned it to the box—isn't that right?"

Ms. Tsuburaya gasped at my words.

When she had shown him into the office earlier that afternoon, he had most likely seized the opportunity to place the book, which he had been keeping in his business bag, into the box while she had gone to fix tea.

Putting back the book was the other reason Tamogami had visited Koumoto Books.

"…Tch, don't show that thing to me." He tried to look away.

I insisted, "No, look at it. And please read it to the end. This book that Emon sent to you contains the answer you'd spent so long waiting for. Please accept it."

He glared back at me stiffly.

But then his gaze shifted slightly to focus on the cover, and the voice of a small boy called out once again to this man whose eyes were full of pain and sorrow.

"Kouichi.

"My papa wrote me after he'd heard from the doctor that Mama would probably never have children…

"He tried to cheer her up and told her it was okay if they didn't have any kids, but…actually, he was really disappointed…

"He was thinking about how Koumoto Books would end with his generation as he wrote me…"

"Emon decided to write this book when his wife miscarried their first child and the doctor told them they could no longer expect to have kids."

Tamogami's shoulders jumped in surprise.

With a painful feeling in my chest, I repeated the words that the childlike voice was telling me with all its might. I described the side of Emon that the adorable little book had seen.

"At the time, Emon had thought Koumoto Books was going to end with his generation, right? And just as his father, Kanesada, had left behind a single painting in the face of death, Emon, too, produced this picture book as he thought about the final days of the store."

It was a way of distracting himself from his sadness.

Because he certainly couldn't allow himself to show his pain in front of his wife.

"As he was writing me, Papa laughed to himself about how bad he was at writing.

"He was chuckling the whole time about how his pictures and words were both awful."

"Emon didn't make this book for anyone else to read. He never wanted to be a writer or anything. He was just trying to sort out his own feelings."

Tamogami had been so tormented by the guilt of his plagiarism because he was a writer before anything else. And he had projected his feelings onto his friend.

That was the source of their misunderstanding.

"If Emon had been on the same path as you, if he were another aspiring writer, then your conduct would have been absolutely unforgivable. He probably would have spoken up, claimed ownership of his creation. But he didn't care about becoming an author. He didn't really care what happened to the story once he was finished writing it."

It didn't matter to him if the book was any good or not.

He was satisfied just to finish it.

"Please read it. Once you do, I'm sure it will be clear to you as well."

"Read me, Kouichi!

"Turn my pages."

With both hands, I held out the little book bound between sheets of cardboard, and I stared at Tamogami. Finally, he took it and slowly opened the front cover.

*   *   *

"There was only one bookstore in the town.

"Once, there had been three, but one by one, they closed, until finally the last one was all alone."

The pictures and prose were crude, like a child had written them.
Tamogami must have been recalling the past as he turned the construction-paper pages. He narrowed his eyes, pain and misery clinging to his face.

"Kouichi, my papa always talked about how amazing you are.

"He was amazed you could turn such a clumsy book like me into such a moving story.

"He would say, 'Kouichi is really incredible.

"'He's a talented, splendid author.'"

Mr. Tamogami could not hear the childlike voice speaking to him from the page written in crayon.
But the voice sounded happy.
As if it couldn't help but be glad to have its pages turned by the "Kouichi" that its "papa" had praised so highly.
In its cute voice, the book continued narrating about how Papa had told it all about Kouichi, how he'd talked about what parts of Kouichi's book he liked, and how he'd always been happy when he read Kouichi's book.
It said Papa loved Kouichi, his treasured friend and an author he admired.
And then, the book suddenly fell quiet in the middle of what it was saying, and its tone of voice saddened.

"Papa said he was sorry.

*   *   *

"While he was preparing to send me to Kouichi, he told me, 'I'm sorry, I should have said something to him earlier.

"'I'm sorry, I'm sorry,' he said.

"'—I'm sorry, Kouichi. I'm sorry.'"

Tamogami shouldn't have been able to hear the book, but still his eyes quickly filled with tears.

And then, after he had finished turning the final page—

—he saw that there was something written on the cardboard cover in felt-tip pen:

I offer this picture book to Mr. Kouichi Tamogami.

Thank you so much for taking this poorly made story and breathing life into it, for conferring it with beautiful color and brilliance.

It only ever made me happy.

"It only ever made me happy…"

That was what Emon had most wanted to convey to Tamogami.

That he was happy about what had happened.

Emon was happy that his clumsy picture book had been transformed into a wonderful piece of art. He was happy that Tamogami had come to hold his book signing at Koumoto Books once he was a published author. He was happy that the customers had excitedly held Tamogami's book in their hands and formed a line so long it stretched out the door.

It had all been so very wonderful and made him so happy he could hardly stand it.

*   *   *

"Emon…!"

Tamogami hugged the little book tightly and started bawling.

In between sobs, he apologized and called his friend's name. Tears poured down his cheeks.

"Kouichi, don't cry.

"Papa loved you, and I love you, so don't cry."

An image floated up in the back of my mind of a little boy stroking Tamogami's head while on the verge of crying himself.

The little boy resembled Emon.

"Mr. Tamogami, you got your big break by plagiarizing Emon's story. But after that, you continued working as an author for over twenty years, all on your own. You should be proud of that. And you should keep on writing after this. That would be the best apology and the best memorial you could give to Emon."

Tamogami was hanging his head and covering his face with both hands. His tear-choked voice had run dry, and he had given himself over to sobbing. Asuka wrapped her arms around his shoulders and hugged him.

His guilt would likely haunt him for a long time. Along with his remorse over lashing out so harshly…

His days of suffering would continue.

Even so, I hoped he would keep writing.

That was Emon's wish, after all.

Ms. Tsuburaya squeezed her hands together fiercely. She was obviously enduring her own sadness and inner turmoil.

Her expression was strained and severe, but she looked frailer than her typically decisive self.

She must have been thinking about Emon.

Thinking about his short life and how he'd lost the people he'd loved one after another.

Thinking about his feelings as he sat in this room alone, the room decorated with a painting called *Extinction*, and wrote his parting words to a dear friend in the back of a handmade picture book...

Perhaps wondering, *Did he suffer? Or was he smiling as always?*

Unable to cry and shout like Tamogami, she bit her lip and bore the sad thoughts alone.

I crossed in front of Ms. Tsuburaya and pulled another book off Emon's bookshelf.

"Emon always seemed a lot like Kolbaba to me."

I spoke quietly, and she opened her eyes wide in amazement.

Because I also wanted to talk about him.

I wanted to talk about him with one of the books he loved, *The Long, Long Story of the Postman*.

"Kolbaba, the character who appears in this book, is a postman. He meets some tiny little people who help him with the sorting in the post office late at night, and they teach him that letters written with feeling will be warm to the touch when handled."

She frowned as she listened to me.

"One day, he gets a letter that has no address and no stamp. He can't deliver a letter without an address, but this one is very warm.

"Kolbaba goes to consult with the little people and asks if they can read the contents of the letter. When one of them presses the letter to his forehead, he sees that written inside is a proposal from a scatterbrained young man named Frankie to a girl named Marie."

"'If you like, we could get married. If you still love me, please reply right away. Don't wait!'"

"Kolbaba decides that this letter absolutely must be delivered, no matter what it takes, and he sets out to do just that."

*   *   *

"'I'm heading out to search for where the young lady lives! Even if it takes me years, even if I have to walk all around the world.'"

"So Kolbaba sets out on a long, long journey. And then, after one year and one day, he's finally able to hand the letter over to Marie."

Emon had been able to understand the feelings of a book by touching its cover with the palm of his hand.
Just like Kolbaba and his letters.
But that was not the only thing they had in common.

"Emon was someone who had always wished from the bottom of his heart to deliver warm books to the people who needed them."

With those kind eyes of his, he told me that a book felt warm when it was happy and that a happy book was a lucky book.
He'd hoped he could make all the books in the store warm.
He'd wanted to give his customers lucky books.

"He told me that even if it took a year and a day or even longer, he wanted to connect people with books like that. And he did. He delivered many books into the hands of the people of this town.

"After his long, long delivery journey ends, Kolbaba says the following—

"'I ran around carrying that letter for a year and a day, you know, but there was value in doing it. For you see, I was able to travel here and there throughout the country and see so many things. I visited Plzeň, Hořice, and even Tabor. My, what a wonderful, beautiful land this is!'"

"Kolbaba is carefree and calm, as if it had been no hardship at all to walk the whole length of the country. He says the beautiful sights made the journey worth it all on its own. If you ask me, Emon Koumoto was just the same."

*   *   *

Bookstores as they exist now are headed on a gentle slope toward extinction, along with paper books.

And Emon himself had lost his parents early and then his wife and child as well. He had been beset by a brain tumor and given only six months to live.

Despite that, he'd smiled gently and promised that he would keep the bookstore going as long as he lived.

With perfectly clear eyes, he continued on, peaceful and relaxed, giving the people who visited his shop warm and happy books.

Becoming the owner of a bookstore was not something Emon had chosen. It was something he'd inherited, a family business.

But he loved books.

And he loved people.

In this tall and slim three-story shop, he was surrounded by warm books, and he met all the customers who came to visit and struck up conversations with them—Emon must have seen many beautiful and lovely scenes.

And I'm sure that he thought to himself—

Thank goodness I became a bookseller.

There was great value in being born in a bookstore and growing up to run the place.

Ms. Tsuburaya looked as if she was holding back tears. She was sitting straight up, pursing her lips as the corners of her eyes grew damp.

She looked lonely yet dignified, like the painting that hung on the wall—a sad, elegant sight.

Tamogami still had Emon's handmade picture book pressed against his chest and was quietly hanging his head. Embracing him, Asuka also had her eyes closed in pain.

And then there were Emon's books, lined up on the shelves.

They were speaking.

Testifying about what kind of person Emon Koumoto had been.

*   *   *

"He had really gentle hands."

"He always handled us with deep affection."

"He was sad, unfortunate, and strong."

"Emon smiled happily as he turned my pages."

"He cried when he read me."

"When he read me, he laughed."

"He flipped through my pages again and again."

"He never forgot about me."

"He was such a warm person."

"He was so kind."

"I loved him."

"I loved it when Emon touched me."

"I wanted to make him feel happy for much longer."

"I wanted Emon to read me one last time."

"I wanted to live a long life as his book."

"I loved him."

"I loved him, too, always."

*   *   *

"I loved him."

"I'm so glad Emon read me."

They sounded just like mourners at a wake, solemnly reminiscing about the deceased.

He was a deeply loving man.

They loved him back.

Reverberating like endless ripples in still water, their voices carried on and on.

The book I was clutching to my chest, *The Long, Long Story of the Postman*, also mumbled sadly in an amiable, masculine voice.

"You know, I...I watched Emon grow up, from the time he was a little child, tottering around... I really loved him. I doubt there's another store owner anywhere who would have loved us so purely and treated us so dearly. I'm glad I was born as a book, since the finest reader around turned my pages."

Surrounded by the books' loving eulogies, Ms. Tsuburaya, Mr. Tamogami, Ms. Asuka, and I all reflected on the Emon Koumoto that we held in each of our hearts.

Mr. Tamogami made an official announcement on his webpage that his famous novel, *A Funeral for Kanoyama Books*, was inspired by the book Emon had written, *The Last Bookstore*. He also uploaded every page of *The Last Bookstore* there for public view.

This ran in the news along with a report about Koumoto Books, the last bookstore open in a small Tohoku town, closing due to the death of its owner. The story quickly spread across the internet and garnered a lot of attention.

So many people tried to buy a copy of *A Funeral for Kanoyama Books* that the physical book ran out of stock and the publisher had to order an emergency reprinting. Sales of the e-book also skyrocketed, putting it in first place that very day.

A television special was put together for the evening news, in which Tamogami promised he would offer all proceeds from subsequent sales of *A Funeral for Kanoyama Books* to help open a new bookstore in town.

And then, it was the final day of business for Koumoto Books.

The store filled with people, and not just locals but also visitors from other prefectures who had heard about the closing on the news and came to visit the bookstore they fondly remembered.

From early in the morning, people came holding books filled with memories of the shop to have their photos taken with their books and make commemorative signs.

Whether they held their book up beside their face and flashed a peace sign or hugged the book tightly, or made a kissing face at it, all the people in the photos beamed in delight.

The pictures filled every flatbed display in the shop, but even that wasn't enough. They were placed all around the register, on the shelves, and even in the bathrooms. It was a magnificent spectacle.

The greatest book in the world!

This book changed my life!

A friend that will last a lifetime!

These words and more were written in pink, blue, and gold pen. But I saw one kind of message more than any other.

I loved Koumoto Books!

I'll never forget Koumoto Books!

Natsu, Kanesada, Emon—thank you so much.

*   *   *

Some customers wiped the corners of their eyes as they read the messages, while others sobbed openly, clutching books to their chests and lamenting that the store was really going away. Other customers saw them cry and started sniffling, too.

But the great majority of the people were smiling, chatting about their memories of Koumoto Books. Their faces were as cheerful as the multicolored pop signs.

Many people purchased a copy of *A Funeral for Kanoyama Books* from a stack beside the register and spoke nostalgically of days past.

"I was here almost twenty years ago for the book signing, too, you know! I wanted to give it another read. Emon looked so happy back then."

A long, long line stretched outside the shop, longer than at the book signing, and the crowd didn't let up for a moment.

Everyone looked happy.

Everyone was smiling.

Even the crying people were soon wearing tearful smiles as they selected new books from the shelves and displays.

Some bought ten books by themselves, and there was even someone who bought fifty and asked that they be delivered to his house. The books that had tightly packed the shelves gradually thinned out.

The other part-timers and I were extremely busy, without a second to rest, but we were in high spirits and didn't feel tired in the slightest.

Ms. Tsuburaya was working harder than anyone.

The day before, I had confided something in her, and she had looked as if she would cry.

"It wasn't just the books that told me you are the most reliable part-timer here, Ms. Tsuburaya. Emon told me that, too. That's why, when we first met, I knew immediately, 'Ah, this woman must be the one he called Minami.'"

Her eyes were still a little red, even now. She must have cried a lot the night before, once she was alone.

But today, the last day that the store was open, she was briskly giving instructions to the other part-time workers and running around herself, serving customers and stocking shelves.

"Ms. Tsuburaya, when you finish there, please go ahead and take a lunch break. There's still plenty of time left before closing," I told her.

Without making a displeased face as she had earlier, she replied, "I'll do that. Thanks."

Before she went on break, she looked around the store and mumbled, "…This is the busiest I've ever seen Koumoto Books since I started working here. Everyone's bringing their favorite books with them to the store, and the whole place is buried in colorful signs… It's just as the boss wrote in *The Last Bookstore*… I wonder if he knew this day was coming…"

Her voice was tinged with an understandable note of sadness.

"Koumoto Books will probably end with my generation."

I recalled Emon's words.

"Just as innumerable creatures have gone extinct or evolved on this earth up until now, I think books and bookstores are probably in the middle of their own evolution."

In a quiet voice, he had told me this matter-of-factly.

"They're destined for extinction, unable to keep living on in their current form…"

After he had mumbled that in a lonely way, he had smiled gently.

I answered Ms. Tsuburaya quietly.

"I think he knew the store would close sometime after he died… And that the town would lose its only bookstore… I think he probably had a hunch about it. That's why he dreamed up the happiest possible ending and tried to write it down, don't you think?"

"The happiest possible…ending?"

*   *   *

"On the day of the funeral, the people of the town gathered at the bookstore.

"Everyone brought a book that held special memories for them.

"And they told one another about their favorite.

"Each person made a sign about their title.

"The signs were many colors—pink, red, blue, yellow, purple—and all together, they looked like a field of flowers.

"'That book was just delightful!'

"'This one really surprised me.'

"'This title, too—I found it quite useful, you know.'

"'I really loved this book.'

"There were many, many, many such words spoken that day.

"The signs swayed in the air above the books, which were all warm and happy.

"And they told one another about their favorite books."

Ms. Tsuburaya took another look around with teary eyes at the field of signs blooming about the store and the customers picking out books while reminiscing with one another happily about Koumoto Books—and she smiled slowly, mumbling something to herself.

"In that case, I think...the boss's dream came true..."

*   *   *

I'm sure you're right.

The thought seemed to draw her heart up from the depths of her grief.

"You know, I think I'm going to lend a hand getting a new bookstore up and running in this town. I think I'd like to keep selling books here."

"When you do, I'll be sure to come."

Books and bookstores, they're both headed for extinction.

But in this moment, in this place, there are still books here.

And there are people selling them.

And people coming to buy them.

It's so busy and bright, you would never think today is the last day, the end of the last bookstore in town.

And—

It was several days after the closing of Koumoto Books.

I was visiting the shop for one last good-bye on the morning I was to return to Tokyo.

The books that remained after the closing fair had all been returned, and the ones that couldn't be returned had been donated or collected by secondhand bookstores. All the shelves in the shop were empty.

It felt lonesome, but it was also a relief—everything was neat and clean.

While he was alive, Emon had made a request of me.

He had asked me to listen to the voices of the books that were left in the store after his death.

And to speak back to them.

"Musubu, you can hear the voices of books and are a good friend to them. So I want you to please give each one my warmest thanks."

That's why I had come to Koumoto Books.

I'd listened carefully to the books that had been Emon's family and friends. Once everyone had gone home each night, I had walked through every corner of the shop by myself and spoken to the books.

*   *   *

"Thank you."

"Good work, everyone."

"Emon and I both hope that wherever you travel after this, there will be some joy waiting for you there."

"Give the people who pick you up and flip through you plenty of amusement, okay? If you do, I'm sure you all will also be happy."

"Never forget that you were once here at Koumoto Books, with an owner who loved you from the bottom of his heart. I want you to be proud of the fact that you come from here."

"Thank you."

"Thank you."

"Take care."

The books also made a subdued fuss.

"Koumoto Books was a very happy place!"

"I'm so glad I was a Koumoto Books book."

"I loved everyone—the owner, Emon, and all the part-timers, too."

"Ms. Natsu and Mr. Kanesada were also wonderful people!"

All of them had been warm without exception.
In the short time that I had been at Koumoto Books, the feelings of so

many titles had touched me, and I had learned the stories of the people who read them.

Of the veterinarian Michijirou and the single picture book that had changed his entire life.

Of Akio and Eiko, tied together through the long years by a novel.

Of Asuka, marching forward with dignity, holding both an old and a new copy of *The Seagull* in her heart.

Of the middle schoolers Hirotaka and Souta, who even now continued to enjoy the Zorori series that Emon had recommended.

Of the long-suffering Tamogami, who had identified with the misdeeds of the minister Dimmesdale in *The Scarlet Letter* and was now finally able to look forward.

Even Ms. Tsuburaya, who carried Emon's prescription, *Alain on Happiness*, with her always and who seemed as if she would someday get her wish.

When I closed my eyes, an image of Emon's smiling face floated up in my mind.

His eyes were narrowed behind his glasses, smiling broadly as he stroked a book gently with his pale palm.

I could almost hear the animated voice of Kanesada, surrounded by children while reading a picture book aloud.

Natsu was watching over him with a stern expression.

And then a little boy who looked like Emon came over, clutching a book to his chest as he tottered along, looking up at his father with big, round eyes.

"Papa, this book is suuuper fun!"

"I love books—I really do!"

"When I grow up, I'm gonna run a bookstore just like you, Papa."

Emon's eyes sparkled as he picked up the little boy, overjoyed. He spoke to his son in a voice overflowing with love and hope.

*   *   *

"The books say that they love, love, love you right back, Mirai. They say they'll be very happy when you're running the store."

Then he rubbed his face against the boy's soft cheek, which smelled of milk, and continued with a smile.

"I want you to read lots of books and get close with them. Every book in this store will become your friend, Mirai."

"Okay, Papa!"

Some people would probably hear the story of the Koumoto family, of Natsu, Kanesada, and Emon, and think they were an unlucky line.

But the Koumotos' story was a long, long one, which I'm sure couldn't be told in full even by all the books and people who'd come through the shop over the years.

Books and bookstores are in the middle of an evolution, and the form in which they currently exist is likely to disappear someday.

Like everything we adore, there will come a day when they are all long gone.

But that is in the future.

In the present, books and bookstores still exist. As long as I'm still alive, I will go on loving books—those heroic, affectionate, and miraculous beings.

And I'll keep on visiting bookstores in order to meet them.

When I opened my eyes, the vision of the Koumoto family disappeared, and the only thing I could see was the empty shelves.

The only person on the quiet sales floor, I stood there for a while holding a copy of *The Field Guide of Extinct Animals*.

This *Field Guide*, the one that had snatched away Emon's life, had been tormented ever since it had been returned from the police station, grieving and moaning.

* * *

"I killed Emon.

"But in the moment of his death, he said this with a smile.

"'Thank you, I loved you all.'"

Just as he had told Tamogami that he had always been happy, Emon had faced the end quietly, without resentment or regrets.

He probably imagined he was going to meet his wife and son.

Up in the sky, he would put the little boy that resembled him so closely up on his knee and turn the pages of a book with gentle hands.

The volume I was holding kept on blaming itself, but I told the tome that it wasn't at fault. It had been telling me all along that it wanted to be thrown away, but when I asked the book to come with me, it responded with a tearful yes. Princess Yonaga, who was always going on about infidelity, was thankfully silent.

I'd better get going over to the station, or I'll miss my train home. The new semester starts the day after tomorrow, and I'll be a second-year then.

Emon had once told me that I was like the tiny little people in the postman's story, but now, like Kolbaba, who sets out on a long, long journey to deliver the warm letter with no address, I had gotten to see the value in spending time at Koumoto Books.

Clutching *The Field Guide of Extinct Animals* tightly to my chest, I turned out the lights and left the store. In my ears, the final words of *The Long, Long Story of the Postman* echoed in Emon's quiet, gentle voice.

"Thus, everybody went home happy.

"And so, this story, too, has now arrived safely at its final destination."

PRINCESS YONAGA'S BONUS CONTENT

...Because I stayed put in Musubu's pocket the entire time!

My moment in the spotlight never came...

(´ ;ω; `)

Musubu...did you forget about me...?

(;≧◇≦)

You're getting worn-out, working for this part-time lady.

Σ(° Д °;)

And you're too friendly toward the customers, too......

(* ` ∧ ´ *)

Musubu mustn't smile at anyone other than me!

ヽ(° ` Д ´ °))

Hey, don't touch other books' covers so gently, either!

o(>_< *)(* >_<)o

No, no, stop, stop! I'm gonna curse you!

o・°・(*/□*)・°・o

......I want to go home soon.

(´ ;Д; `)

AFTERWORD

I was raised in a large city in Tohoku. When I was growing up, it was so prosperous that there were three department stores right in front of the train station, and it was easy to find good books.

My neighborhood had a splendid central library, there were bookstores everywhere, and all of them were packed to the brim with people picking out things to read. All the new releases would be lined up for display the day before they went on sale, and I would set out cheerfully for the bookstore to make my purchases.

The busiest of all the bookstores was a three-story building in the shopping arcade near the station. It was basically a reader's paradise, with books densely lining the shelves almost all the way up to the ceiling. Whenever we went out as a family, my mother would always take my little brother along with her to shop. While they were gone, my father and I would wait for them and read.

My father would head for the corner on the first floor where they kept the magazines and paperbacks. I would stick to the children's section on the second floor, and I would feel so happy and fortunate whenever my dad would buy me a book on the way out.

As I grew up, I started going to the manga section on the third floor as well, and I really got to read so many books. I fondly remember the days when bookstores were more tolerant of people standing around and reading.

The books I was looking for and the books I wanted—all of them were there in that store. I cannot recall a single instance of a book being sold out or not available for purchase because it hadn't been delivered. I was always confident that if I went there, they would have any kind of book I might want. It was a point of pride for me that our town had a bookstore like that.

Even after I moved to Tokyo for university, in my mind, that bookstore was still the best around. Internally, I was so proud of it. *The bookstore in my hometown is so amazing! It's the best in Tohoku—no, the best in all of Japan!*

When I learned that that bookstore would be closing, I really couldn't believe it. I cried and sobbed while searching the internet for more information. I couldn't imagine that such a successful bookstore, loved by all the locals, could just disappear. I had always thought that at least the bookstore would be right there forever, unchanging.

The whole time I was writing this story about Koumoto Books, I was reminiscing about that space where I felt nothing but happiness.

The story of the people who ran Koumoto Books ends here, but Musubu's story is going to be sold simultaneously under the Famitsu Bunko publishing label. It's a collection of short stories, titled *Bond and Book: The Devotion of "The Surgery Room."* All sorts of books will make their appearance. Please consider reading it alongside this volume.

The illustrations for both books are courtesy of Miho Takeoka. When I received the cover for this book and saw the clean drawing of Natsu, Emon, and Kanesada from the back, I was so moved that I started to cry. Once you finish reading this book, please take your book cover off and take another look at the three of them.

Finally, I want to say that no matter what changes the future will bring for books and bookstores, I'm certain their essential qualities will be the same. And I will always, always love them.

May 29, 2020   *Mizuki Nomura*

The following works are quoted or referenced in this book.

Tomb of the Wild Chrysanthemum; Itō Sachio (Shinchosha)

The Seagull & Uncle Vanya; Anton Chekhov, author;
Kiyoshi Jinzai, translator (Shinchosha)

The Scarlet Letter; Nathaniel Hawthorne, author;
Toshio Yagi, translator (Iwanami Shoten)

Kaiketsu Zorori and the Mysterious Aliens; Yutaka Hara
(Poplar Publishing)

Alain on Happiness; Émile-Auguste Chartier (Alain), author;
Kenzō Shirai, translator (Shueisha)

The Long, Long Story of the Postman; Karel Čapek, author;
Akane Kurisu, translator (Kaizansha)

BOND & BOOK

The **Devotion** of "The **Surgery Room**"

Mizuki Nomura

ILLUSTRATION BY
Miho Takeoka

New from Yen On!

Musubu Enoki is an ordinary high schooler with an extraordinary ability—he can hear the voices of books. When he happens to notice one lost and crying, the young man sets out to reunite a children's classic with its original owner. Musubu leaves no page unturned in his quest to assist tomes of all sorts, including "The Surgery Room" by classic Japanese author Kyōka Izumi. But can this advocate for books really make their dreams come true?!

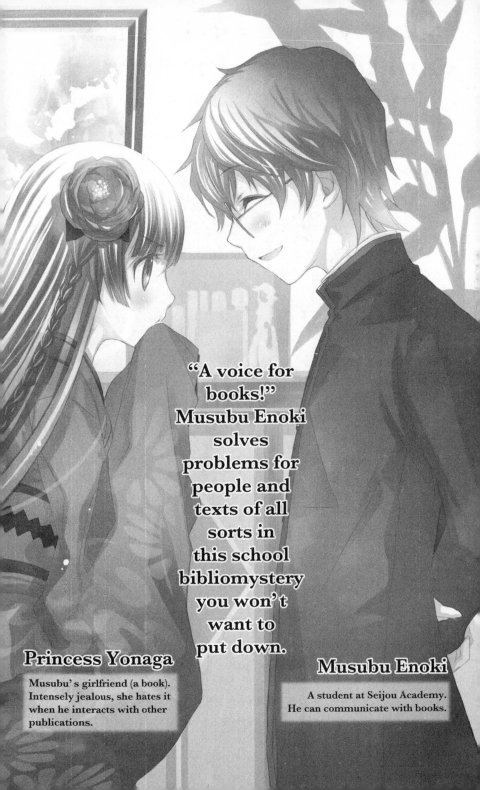

"A voice for books!" Musubu Enoki solves problems for people and texts of all sorts in this school bibliomystery you won't want to put down.

Princess Yonaga
Musubu's girlfriend (a book). Intensely jealous, she hates it when he interacts with other publications.

Musubu Enoki
A student at Seijou Academy. He can communicate with books.